MURDER

and

MAYHEM

IN CEDAR FALLS

MURDER

and

MAYHEM

IN CEDAR FALLS

WALTER WITTMUSS

ARPress
45 Dan Road Suite 5
Canton MA 02021

Hotline: 1(888) 821-0229
Fax: 1(508) 545-7580

Ordering Information:

Quantity sales. Special discounts are available on quantity purchases by corporations, associations, and others. For details, contact the publisher at the address above.

Printed in the United States of America.

ISBN-13:   Softcover   979-8-89356-935-3
                eBook   979-8-89356-936-0

Library of Congress Control Number: 2023920954

CONTENTS

"Ten miles to Cedar Falls," the road sign said.

Ten miles closer to a new life, I told myself as I drove down the two-lane state highway in my vintage Cadillac convertible. *A new job, a new town, a new life...*

The green countryside of cornfields, soybean fields, and lush green pastures filled with herds of dairy cows flashed by on either side of the highway. The fifty-five-mile-an-hour wind whipped my brown hair. The rolling hills of the Midwest was a refreshing change from the flat terrain of North Texas.

Then ten minutes later, a sign proclaiming "Cedar Falls" came into view. I slowed down as I entered the Cedar Fall's town limits. Another sign directed me where to turn to find Duncan College. I drove past nice, tidy houses with well-kept lawns.

A large three-story building of gray stone came into view. A curved half-circle drive with parking slots graced the area between the building and the street. Bushes and a large sign reading "DUNCAN COLLEGE" in bold letters and "Administration Building" in smaller letters filled the space between the street and drive. I turned into the drive, drove up to the building, and parked in one of the slots. I grabbed my briefcase and patted my Cadillac affectionately as I exited it. I climbed the Administration Building's steps.

As was the case in most hollowed halls of universities, colleges, or other institutions of higher education, it would have been dreary and oppressive but for the modern ceiling lights, which helped to a degree. Silence hung like a heavy cloud in the building's interior. Most of the office doors I could see had light shining through their frosted windows. I picked the office that had "Chancellor" written on its glass in black letters. I knocked.

A female's voice told me to come in. I opened the door to find myself in an outer office with a good-looking middle-aged woman seated behind an uncluttered desk.

"May I help you, sir?" she inquired sweetly.

"Maybe. I'm Professor Brennon. I wanted to let the proper people know I had arrived."

"I don't quite understand, Professor," she said, puzzled.

"I am the new astronomy professor. I have a letter in my briefcase that would explain everything if you would like to see it."

"No, that won't be necessary. Pretty much everybody knows you are coming, but just a few know what your name is. Let me be the first to welcome you to Duncan College. Now, you need to go to the dean's office. He is the one who takes care of the academic part. His office is four doors down and to the right of our office. And good luck, Professor."

"Thank you very much, and you have a nice day."

I stepped out of the office. My footsteps echoed on the highly polished tile floor. I went past the Admissions Office, the Boys' Guidance Counselor's Office, and the Girls' Guidance Counselor's Office before coming upon the Dean's Office. I knocked and again was told to enter. A younger and pretty girl sat behind a desk, brightening my day.

"Yes, sir. What can I do for you?" she asked.

"I'm Professor Brennon. I'm heading up the Astronomy Department. I just got into town and wanted to check in."

"Oh, Professor Brennon," she said in a warm voice. "We've been expecting you. Please have a seat, and I'll let Dean Hawks know that you have arrived." Then she said into the intercom, "Mr. Hawks,

Professor Brennon is here to see you." After a short pause, she turned back to me. "You can go in now, Professor."

"Thank you," I said.

"Professor Brennon," Dean Hawks said with gusto when I entered his office. He stood up and stretched out his hand as I approached his desk. I shook his offered hand. "It's a pleasure to finally meet you in person after all the correspondence. I hope you had a good trip?"

"Yes, sir. It was a long drive but a good one."

"You didn't have any trouble finding Cedar Falls?"

"No, sir. It was right where the map said it would be."

"Yes," he said a little dryly. Apparently, he didn't appreciate my brand of humor all that much. "Have you gotten your living arrangements worked out, or do you need some assistance on finding something?"

"Thank you for the offer of assistance, but I had an uncle pass away recently, and he left me his house and property in town. I will be living there."

"Good. The first semester starts in three weeks. Will that be enough time for you to get all your supplies and teaching material in?"

"I believe so. If I understand your letter correctly, Mr. Hawks, I will be starting this department from scratch."

"You understand it correctly, Professor Brennon. The great-granddaughter of the college founder, just like he did, has a very deep interest in astronomy. She feels that with all the advances in space exploration, astronomy is a very important subject. Since she is the chairperson on the school's board of regents, she can add the course to the college's curriculum. While it was her great-grandfather that built the observatory, it was her who has had the most modern telescope installed in it. Here are the keys to your classroom and to the observatory. If there is anything else I can help you with, just let me know."

"Thank you very much, Mr. Hawks. The only other thing I need right now is a map of the campus."

"You can get one in the Admissions Office."

"One other thing. To whom and where do I turn in my list of supplies?"

"All school supplies are ordered and picked up at the Maintenance Building. Just look for the receiving counter, and they will explain the procedure to you. If there is nothing else, have a good day, Professor."

"And you, too, Mr. Hawks."

I left Dean Hawks's office and went to the Admissions Office. They were able to provide me with a map of the town as well as a map of the campus.

I left the cool interior of the building and stepped out into the early August hot sun. I put my briefcase on the front seat beside me after getting into the car. The seat was fairly hot, so I raised the top and turned on the air conditioner. The interior cooled down quickly while I studied the town map.

My uncle's house was only three blocks from the college campus. I left the campus to go to my new lodgings. I found the address and pulled into the driveway.

I double-checked the address to make sure I was at the right house. It was a lot bigger than I had expected, but I never knew Uncle Jeremy very well either. It appeared he had done very well for himself. I was surprised when I was informed that he had left his property to me. Of course, part of the reason might have been because my mother and he had been very close from the time they were kids up until he died. He had never married. Thus, he had no kids of his own to leave it to.

It was a large one-story red-brick structure with white trim, a ranch-style house. A three- stall attached garage was behind the house. There was also a small shed on the property.

I let myself into the house with the key my uncle's lawyer had given me. Just as the lawyer had said, the house was fully furnished. The furniture was all of excellent quality. A quick tour revealed a living room, a spacious kitchen, a master bedroom, two smaller bedrooms, and an office or den, whichever I wanted to use it as. The refrigerator and cupboards were empty, so I figured the first order of business would be to get some food in the house.

I grabbed the phone book and looked up the listings of grocery stores in the town. When I found one I thought I would like, I located where it was on the town map. I locked up the house, jumped into my car, and started out in search of the grocery store.

About four blocks from my house, I was checking a street sign while entering an intersection when out of the corner of my eye, I caught the flash of a white car also entering the intersection. I jammed on my brakes but not quite fast enough. With a resounding crash, my car jolted to a stop against the front fender of the white car.

A woman with long black hair about my age was behind the wheel of the white car. She shook her head to clear it. Then she leaped from her car and rushed toward my car before I had much of a chance to get out of my car.

"What is the matter with you?" she yelled, waving her arms. "You were looking up at the wild blue yonder instead of watching where you were driving this tank?" She slapped the hood of the Caddy.

"Hold on. Hold on," I implored, holding up my hands in a gesture of surrender as I walked to the front of my car. "I'm very, very sorry. I realize this is all my fault. I have insurance, and here is my driver's license and registration," I said, handing everything to her.

"This is a Texas driver's license and a Texas address. How am I going to get in touch with you, if need be, after you go on your merry way?" she asked me as she handed me her license, proof of insurance, and registration.

"Gee, I don't know. I guess you will just have to run me down."

She quickly looked up at me to see if I was serious. I didn't think she could quite make up her mind if I was or not.

"And I see your plates are Texas plates," she said in despair.

"Yes, they are, Miss….or is it Mrs. Cole?"

"I don't know why I should tell you, but it's Miss Cole. And this is my only transportation."

Just then a police car pulled up and parked at the curb. A young officer—he couldn't have been any more than twenty-five or twenty-six years old—got out of the police car and came over to inspect the accident damage.

"Hello, Denise. Had a fender bender, I see."

"I'm afraid I ran into her, Officer," I said quickly.

"And your name, sir?" officer Hollister asked.

"John Brennon. Miss Cole is holding my license, proof of insurance, and registration."

The deputy took my documents from Denise and started looking them over. "Is this your current address, Mr. Brennon?" he asked.

"No," I answered while smiling at Denise. "My current address as of today is 1021 Fifth Street, Cedar Falls, Nebraska. I just got into town this morning, so naturally, I haven't had time to change anything."

"Okay. I will have to give you a ticket for not yielding the right of way. You also have thirty days in which to change your driver's license and plates."

"That's fine, Officer. I'll be sure to take care of everything in a timely manner."

Denise kept her eyes on me as her friend—or I assumed he was a friend because of the way he had addressed her—wrote out my ticket. I signed the ticket, and the deputy left after asking Denise if she needed a tow truck. We looked her car over, and she decided she could drive it to her garage.

"I'll follow you to the garage that you take your car to and then run you to wherever you need to go," I offered.

"That's okay. I'm sure you have other things to do. I'll be fine."

"Please, let me make amends to you, Miss Cole. It's the least I can do."

"Well, okay, I guess. And call me Denise. I noticed your car isn't damaged except for a small scratch on the bumper."

"Like you said, this car is built like a tank. Shall we go?"

We got into our respective vehicles, and I followed her to Miracle Auto Repair. She was in the garage for fifteen or twenty minutes. She came out and got in my car.

"You really have this in pristine condition," she said as she looked over the interior.

"I have always had a great admiration for this year Cadillac. When I was lucky enough to find one in reasonable condition, I bought it and fixed it up to put it in prime condition. The gas mileage isn't anything to brag about, but I don't care. It's a great car to drive. Would you like to go someplace and have a cup of coffee? Or did you have someplace else you had to go or someplace you had to be at?"

"I haven't any plans that can't be changed. A cup of coffee would taste good. Jim's Cafe has the best coffee in town. I'll direct you to it since you probably don't know your way around town yet."

Following her directions took us to a small building with "Jim's Cafe" written on one of its windows. We got out of my car and went in. I slid in on one side, and Denise slid in on the other side of an empty booth.

"Now, Mr. Brennon…" she started to say after the waitress brought our coffee.

"John. Please call me John," I pleaded, interrupting her.

"Okay, John. Why did you let me rant and rave about Texas when you knew you would be living right here in town?"

"I apologize, Denise. My philosophy on life is to not get too excited about the little things in life. Lord knows there is enough of the big things to get excited about. Besides, I was having a little fun at your expense. I'm sorry if you feel I was underhanded in my actions."

"Wellll…" she said with a straight face but then burst out laughing. "Forget it, John. I guess I flew off the handle a little bit, but I had just gotten that car a couple of months ago. I promise I'm no longer angry. I thought an older guy lived at that address you gave Ben."

"Ben? You mean the deputy?"

"Yes, the deputy."

"My uncle Jeremy Cooper did live there. He passed on a month ago. He left the house and property to me."

"I don't mean to be nosy, but do you have any employment lined up yet?"

"Yes, as a matter of fact, I do. I'm heading up the new Astronomy Department at the college."

"Really! I happen to be a professor in the Music Department at the college."

"Great! That means we will be seeing each other around campus. You realize you are my first friend—that is, if you will have me as your friend—in town," I said, extending my hand across the table.

"Friend it is, as long as you promise not to run into me again when I get my car back," she replied, taking my hand and shaking it. "Now I had better be on my way. I have the little matter of reporting the accident to my insurance, and you definitely have to notify your insurance. By the way, the garage said it will take about a week to fix my car."

"I assume you want to go home?" I asked as we exited the cafe.

"Yes, sir," she replied.

She directed me to her house, which was on the opposite side of town from the college. It was an average-sized two-story house with white frame and slate-gray trim. It had a porch with a swing hanging on it, which was the perfect sitting area for them long, lazy summer evenings. A chain-link fence enclosed a small green yard. I pulled up in the short driveway, stopped, and jumped out to open the car door for Denise.

"Do you live by yourself, Denise, or am I getting too nosy now?"

"No, I don't mind you asking, John," she said with a very pleasant, upbeat voice. "I live with my mother and my German shepherd dog, Shadow. Do you like dogs?"

"Yes, I do. Dogs and I get along fine."

We got to the front door. Denise pushed the door open. Shadow started to bound out of the door to greet Denise. He stopped on a dime when he saw me. He fixed his dark eyes on me, trying to make up his mind whether I was friend or foe.

"It's okay, Shadow," Denise said, petting him. "This is a friend. Come on in, John. He won't do any more than tear your leg off."

"That's what I'm afraid of," I replied jokingly as I stepped through the doorway. I eased my hand down, palm up, toward Shadow. He sniffed my hand then turned back to Denise.

"Is that you, dear?" a mature woman's voice called out from another room.

"Yes, Mom. Come into the living room, please. I would like you to meet someone."

A brunette came out of another room and into the living room. She had a full figure, but not an overweight figure. I felt a warmth radiate from her that put me instantly at ease. She had a stature about her that also demanded respect.

"Mom, I would like you to meet Mr. Brennon. He is a new professor at the college."

"You might say I ran into her downtown today," I said, sticking out my hand. "And I'm very happy to meet you, Mrs. Cole."

She shook my hand with a firm grasp. She swung her eyes back and forth between Denise and me when we both softly chuckled.

"He actually did run into my car today, Mom, literally," Denise explained.

"Are you hurt, dear?" her mother asked, instantly anxious.

"No, Mom, I'm fine. The car has a few wounds, but I'm fine."

"I'm sorry, but I have to run, ladies. It was very nice meeting you, Mrs. Cole. Since this semester hasn't started yet, do you have things you need to get done at the college before classes start, Denise?"

"Yes. I'll be busy most every day."

"Oh, dear," her mother said in a worried voice. "How are you going to get there with no car?"

"It isn't that far, Mom. I'll just walk."

"Honey, don't you realize how dangerous that would be for you? That maniac hasn't been caught yet."

"Maniac?" I asked, stepping back into the house. "I just got into town today, Mrs. Cole. What is this about a loose maniac?"

"Well, Mr. Brennon, over the last couple of months, there has been several women attacked and raped. The first two victims survived. Unfortunately, the last one didn't. There has also been a dog killed just a couple of days ago in the very same manner as the last rape victim."

"Mom, I will be walking in broad daylight. Nobody would be fool enough to try to kidnap or kill someone in broad daylight."

"What time do you usually go in, Denise?" I asked.

"I like to get there at eight o'clock or at least close to it."

"I will be here at quarter to eight to pick you up."

"I can't let you go out of your way like that, John."

"Mrs. Cole, sit on her if you have to tomorrow morning until I pick her up. Okay?"

"Okay, John. Thank you. It would worry me to death to have her walking."

Denise's mother followed me with her eyes as I walked out to my car. After I had left, she turned to Denise.

"How did he manage to run into you, dear?"

"He wasn't watching where he was going. He smacked into my car in an intersection. My car was still drivable, so he followed me over to the garage and then brought me home."

"He seems like a very nice guy."

"I agree. He does seem like a real nice guy. He just got into town this morning."

"I suppose he is staying in the motel until he can find someplace to rent."

"No. As a matter of fact, he will be living in Jeremy Cooper's house over on Fifth Street."

"Jeremy Cooper? Didn't he die just not too long ago?"

"Yes, he did. John is Jeremy's nephew, and Jeremy left the house and property to John."

"Well, your professor friend fell into a sweet deal there. I hope he turns out to be as good as my first impression of him is. Come and help me get supper on now."

I left Denise's house and headed back uptown. I still had to get them groceries that I had started out to pick up when I ran into Denise. I didn't have any problem finding the grocery store because I had passed it while taking Denise home. It was a big enough store that it had a good variety of products. I got what I needed home and put the items away in the cupboard and refrigerator.

I then settled down with the phone. I reported the accident to my insurance company and put in a change of address while I had them on the line. I also called the courthouse to find out the time when they would open and where I had to go in the building to change my driver's license and register my car for this county. There wasn't time to do either one of them things now before they closed. Taking care of them two things would be my first order of business tomorrow morning after taking Denise to the college. The rest of the afternoon and evening I spent getting settled in and relaxing. It had been along day, and tomorrow was going to be a busy day, so I went to bed early.

"Good morning, Denise," I said after she climbed into my car the following morning. "I'm glad to see you took your mother's advice and didn't walk."

"I thank you for the ride, but I don't want you to feel you have to take me everywhere either."

"Friends, remember? Friends do things for friends," I reminded her.

"Right. Friends. I promise to keep that in mind," she said with a big smile.

She directed me to the Music Building. When she got out of the car, I told her I would pick her up at the end of the day to take her home. She told me when she would be done. The courthouse was a large stately gray stone building. It had to be close to eighty years old, judging from its architecture. I parked, and following directions given to me over the phone, I found myself in a short line of four people standing in front of a window marked "Driver's License." The two people in front of me were a couple of middle-aged women.

"What's this world coming to, Rose? You read about that in the paper about that dog that was killed three days ago, didn't you?"

"Yes, and it just made me sick. Who in their right mind would slit a poor dog's throat from ear to ear? Things like that just don't happen in Cedar Falls."

"You hit the nail on the head when you said *right mind*. Nobody in their right mind would do a thing like that. What scares me so bad is, if you remember, that was how that poor girl was killed that was raped not too long ago."

"My husband won't let me go anyplace unless I have a friend go with me."

"I just wonder if the sheriff is making any progress in any of the rape cases. And now there's this dog thing…"

"Your guess is as good as anybody's. If he is, he isn't letting anybody else know."

"All I've got to say is, he had better get his butt in gear. Elections for sheriff is coming up, and if he wants to keep his job, he had better start showing some results."

The two people who had been in front of the two ladies had been taken care of, and now it was Rose's turn. They got through the procedure, and then it was my turn.

"Mr. Brennon," the clerk said, looking at my Texas license, "have you permanently moved to this county?"

"Yes. I've moved from Texas to right here in this town."

"Okay. Have you gotten a permanent address in town yet?"

"Yes, sir. It is 1021 Fifth Street."

"Okay. Since this license isn't expired, the state and county allow me to let your Nebraska license expire on the same date as your Texas license would have. Take this over to have your picture taken," he said, handing me the form he had just filled out. "They will issue you your Nebraska license there. Thank you."

"Thank you," I said, taking the form.

I went over and had my picture taken. Shortly afterward, I had my new license. Next stop was to get new plates for the car. By the time I got everything done, the morning was pretty well gone. I decided to grab a bite to eat over at Jim's Cafe.

I noticed the police patrol car out in front of the cafe. When I walked in, I saw the deputy that knew Denise was seated at a back table. I went over to his table.

"Hello, Deputy. Do you mind if I join you?"

"No, I don't mind. Aren't you the guy that ran into Denise yesterday?"

"Guilty," I admitted with a little laugh. "I got my driver's license and car plates taken care of this morning. I will be happy to show them to you if you like."

The waitress came over with a glass of water. I ordered lunch.

"That won't be necessary. I believe you," the deputy said.

"I am curious about something, Deputy. I know it probably isn't any of my business, but I heard some people talking about three rapes that has happened in town. I also heard a dog was found with its throat cut."

"What about them?"

"Since I'm going to be living in town now, the stories make me a little nervous. I was wondering if the police has made any progress in any of the cases?"

"Not much progress, but of what interest would it be to you, Mister…?"

"Brennon. John Brennon. I just hate to see any criminal escape justice. My profession is astronomy, but I have an interest in crime detection."

"Well, I'm sure Sheriff Blocker will get to the bottom of it and catch the guy doing it all."

"I assume Sheriff Blocker collected DNA from the rape victims?"

"You would have to ask the sheriff. But if he did, it's not much good unless you can find a match, and if that had happened, there would be someone behind bars. The jail is empty. I have to go. Been nice chatting with you, Mr. Brennon."

My lunch came as the deputy left. I ate my hamburger, soup, fries, and Coke. The hot August sun beat down on me as I stepped out of the cafe and walked to my car. The Cadillac's air conditioner kept me cool, though, as I drove to the college. I found the building my classroom was in with the aid of the campus map.

A short distance from the classroom building, on the crest of a hill, stood the imposing observatory. It's high-arched roof with its slit for the telescope, which was now closed, sent a thrill through me. I could vividly see in my mind's eye the wonders of the heavens just waiting to be enjoyed via the telescope.

It surprised me when I thought I saw the figure of a person by the observatory wall. Since classes hadn't started yet, I didn't see what business anybody would have by the observatory. Of course, it could be a cleaning crew person, I reasoned. The figure momentarily stepped out of the shadow of the observatory. I could distinguish that it was a man's, or a boy's, figure. Then just as quickly, the figure disappeared behind the observatory. I wondered whether I should go up and check it out. After a minute or two of debating on what I should do, I decided if the person was a trespasser, the college's security would handle it.

I went into the classroom building and found the room that was to be my classroom. Stepping into the room, I was struck by the bareness of the room. Whatever had been taught in the classroom before was no longer evident. As a matter of fact, the room looked like it hadn't been used for a couple of years. The floor was swept, but there was a thin layer of dust on my desk and on the four tiers of students' seats. As I started to make a list of things I would have to order, like charts, models, and reference books, Denise walked in.

"Hello," I said, surprised. "I had planned on picking you up at the Music Building."

"What I wanted to get done today I finished early, so after finding out where they had put you, I decided to come over and see your new classroom."

"Well, this is it. I haven't been up to the observatory yet. I'm anxious to, though. How long have you been a professor here at the college, Denise?"

"Three years. Why?"

"Is there any reason that you can think of for anybody to be up by the observatory? Maybe a member of the housekeeping staff who cleans the classrooms and maybe the observatory as well?"

"As far as I know, nobody has set foot inside the observatory for a year. Were you able to see the person well enough to describe them?"

"No. I could tell it was a guy, but that is all."

"Well, it wasn't her then."

"Her?"

"Yes. Miss Florence Duncan. The great-granddaughter of the college's founder. She lives in that mansion that sits a little ways from the observatory. But you said it was a guy you saw."

"Yes, it was. When was the new telescope installed?"

"About a year ago. At the time, I thought it was just a waste of money since there wasn't anybody here who really knew how to use it. Are they hard to operate? That size, I mean."

"No, they aren't hard to operate once you know how, but you do have to be trained to operate one. You are saying, though, that nobody has operated the telescope or done any type of maintenance on it since it was installed?"

"I'm not saying no, just none that I know of."

"If that's the case, I hope it hasn't been ruined from neglect. I think I have my list pretty complete. Are you ready to go?"

"Whenever you are."

"I have to stop at the Maintenance Building to turn in this list. Do you mind?"

"No, not at all."

I followed her out, locking the door behind me. When we stepped out of the building, I instinctively looked up toward the observatory. There was nobody there. My eyes slid over to the Duncan Mansion. Denise's eyes followed mine up to the mansion.

Chapter

TWO

"It's a big old place, isn't it?" Denise remarked.

"It is big. Have you ever heard how old it really is?"

"I have heard that the mansion was built by Horance Duncan, the college's founder. That would make the mansion's age somewhere in the neighborhood of eighty to a hundred years old. I would love to see the inside of it once."

"Does Florence Duncan make her presence felt around campus much?"

"Not that much. She stays pretty much up in the mansion except when she has board meetings and such. She has to attend them. She is the chairperson of the board of regents."

"Do you know if she ever married?"

"Not that I know of."

"That large a house would have to get pretty lonesome for her, I would think. Judging from what you just told me, though, I believe a lot of the lonesomeness she might be experiencing now she probably has brought onto herself."

"I suppose so, but I have to feel a little sorry for her," Denise said sadly. "Well, if you want to get that list turned in today yet, we had better be on our way. The Maintenance Building closes at five, and it is four-forty now."

We got in the car and drove to the Maintenance Building. I looked for and found the receiving counter. A young man was behind the counter. He looked up and smiled when I approached the counter.

"Yes, sir. What can I do for you?"

"I'm Professor Brennon from the Astronomy Department, and I was told that this is where I order any supplies I need and also pick the supplies up here."

"You were told right, Professor. I assume you have a list that you need ordered now?"

"Yes, I do."

I fished the list out of my pocket and handed it to him. He looked it over, nodding as he did.

"Do you have any idea how long it will take to get them items?" I asked.

"No, sir, I don't, and the guy that could give you an idea of how long it will take has already left for the day. You could call tomorrow, and he could probably give you an idea."

"I'll do that. Thank you."

"Sure, and welcome to Duncan College, Professor."

I took Denise home, walking her up to the door. We agreed that I would pick her up the following morning and then said good night. I drove home and had a sandwich for supper. I was feeling restless and decided to go for a short walk.

The first couple of houses had wide-open front yards. The third house had five-and-a- half-foot-high hedges that ran from the sidewalk to the backyard. The hedge also stretched across the front to the driveway.

As I walked, flanked by the hedge, my boots made slow thumping sounds on the concrete sidewalk. Then just for an instant, I thought I heard the sounds of struggling. I stopped and listened closely for the sound to repeat itself in the still evening air. I heard the sound a second time. It was coming from the other side of the hedge. I ran down to the driveway and turned into it. As I rounded the end of the hedge, a large figure, dressed all in black, was rising from the ground.

"Help!" a girl's terrified voice screamed out from the ground.

The black figure bolted toward the backyard along the hedge. "Stop! Stop!" I yelled at the fleeing figure. The figure kept on running.

I decided I had better see if the girl had been hurt instead of going after her attacker. Just as I knelt down, the door of the house flew open, spilling light out into the yard.

"What's going on out here?" the voice of an older man behind me gruffly demanded.

"Call the police! A girl has been assaulted in your front yard. Her attacker is getting away," I said quickly.

"What? A girl attacked?" the man stammered.

"Yes. Call the police. Now!"

The man disappeared back inside the house. I put my arms around the girl and helped her to a sitting position. She was sobbing hysterically.

"It's okay, Miss. Your attacker is gone. The police are coming. It's okay. You're safe now," I said to her softly in the most reassuring manner that I could.

As I cradled her shaking body, two police cars, an ambulance, and a fire truck arrived with sirens screaming and lights flashing. Police and firemen converged on the girl in my arms and me. Gently the paramedics took the girl from me and laid her down on the gurney. The sheriff himself came over and tapped me on the shoulder, motioning for me to follow him. I followed him to his patrol car.

"Get in," he said. I got in the car. "Your name?" he began.

"John Brennon."

"Address?"

"1021 South Fifth Street. Three houses down."

"Your place of employment?"

"Professor at the college."

"What happened tonight?"

"I started out for a walk. I got up by the hedge, and I thought I heard a scuffling sound. I stopped to listen, and I heard it again. I ran down to the driveway and ran around the end of the hedge. A figure clothed all in black had already stood up and took off when he saw me in the driveway."

"Can you describe him?"

"About all I can say is that the guy—I assume a guy because of what he was probably trying to do—was at least six foot tall, maybe a little taller. Like I already said, he was dressed entirely in black. I would say he weighed around 220 to 240 pounds. It was hard to get a good estimate of his height and weight in this low light. Even though his face was covered, I could tell he was white from his mouth, nose, and eye holes."

"Did he limp or anything like that when he ran?"

"No. His run was steady and quite normal for the very short time that I did see him run. He was also very fast."

"Did he say anything when you came around the hedge?"

"Not a word. He just took off. I just hope the girl will be okay. Hopefully, she might be able to tell you something about his voice— that is, if he said anything to her."

"Oh, she'll be questioned as soon as she can be. Luckily, it looks like he didn't get the job done."

"Will you be testing for DNA on her?"

"Since it looks like she wasn't raped, there isn't any reason to do any DNA test on her."

"No, I suppose not."

"You said you are a professor at the college, right?"

"Yes."

"What subject do you teach at the college?"

"Astronomy."

"Was you ever a police officer or connected with law enforcement in any capacity?"

"No. Why do you ask?"

"Generally, I am a pretty good judge of character. Some of your answers gave me the impression that you had worked for the law in the past. Apparently, I am off the mark when it comes to you, though."

"Yes and no, Sheriff. I was talking to one of your deputies— Ben, I believe, his name is—the other day in Jim's Cafe. I happen to mention to him that I have an interest in crime solving. I used to live in Texas, and I was able to help the local police solve a crime or two," I explained.

"I don't want to appear heavy-handed or arrogant, but I think my deputies and I will be able to handle this problem. So I am just asking you nicely not to get involved."

"Oh, I promise not to mess up your investigation, Sheriff, but isn't it true this makes four girls and one dog that has been attacked so far with one girl and the dog dead?"

"Unfortunately, that is true, but we are getting closer to catching the maniac."

"I'm glad to hear that, Sheriff. Is there anything else you want me for?"

"No. You can go. I would like you to come down to the police station sometime tomorrow to give a statement."

"I'll be there."

We exited his car, and he went over to where a deputy was looking the scene over. The ambulance and fire truck had already left. The sheriff and his deputy searched the front yard and side yard with their flashlights, looking for anything to help them. I stood by the patrol car and watched them. Finally, they appeared to be satisfied. The deputy walked to his car, and the sheriff came over to his car.

"Was there something else I can do for you, Professor?"

"No. *No.* I was just leaving."

I walked back to my house after the sheriff left. I turned in early. I was exhausted.

A dark form sat with ease in a thickly leafed tree that set at a position that allowed the form to observe what was happening in the yard he had just fled from. He gloated to himself at how inept the police of this town was. He had already enjoyed three other girls before, and the police didn't have the least idea who he was.

I could have had my fourth girl tonight if it wasn't for that busybody who interrupted me by coming around that hedge, he angrily thought. *But there will be another day.*

He watched the police scour the yard; he had complete confidence that they would find nothing. Finally, the police were done and left. He watched the busybody walk off too. After ten minutes or so, he skillfully lowered himself out of the tree with the minimum amount of noise.

Then like a shadow, he silently made his way through the neighborhood to his car, which he had parked several blocks away. Quickly he stripped the black outfit off with practiced ease, stuffing it into an overnight bag. He threw the bag into the trunk of the car then slid behind the wheel.

Just then a patrol car slowly turned the corner. When the patrol car's headlights picked him out sitting in his car, the officer pulled up beside him and stopped.

"Have you seen anybody on the street in the neighborhood tonight dressed all in black?" the officer asked.

"No, sir. I sure haven't. Is the person dangerous?"

"He could be. If you should see anybody dressed like that and acting suspicious, phone the police."

"I certainly will, Officer. And good luck catching him."

After the patrol car left, he burst out laughing. He chuckled all the way home.

The next morning, I got up and grabbed some toast and coffee for breakfast. I had my hand on the car door when I hesitated. I looked at my watch. I had time to go up to the house where the girl was attacked last night and have a little look around before having to pick Denise up. The owner of the house happened to be out in the front yard when I got up there.

"Good morning, sir," I said as I walked up the driveway.

"Good morning. Aren't you that guy that chased that other guy out of my yard last night?"

"Yes, sir. My name is John Brennon. I'm your new neighbor three houses down that way," I said, pointing.

"That would be Jeremy Cooper's house, isn't it?"

"Jeremy was my uncle. As you probably know, he passed away a month ago, leaving me the house and property. And your name, sir?"

"George McAllister."

"I'm very happy to meet you. May I call you George?"

"Certainly. We are going to be neighbors."

"I'm surprised you didn't hear anything last night until that girl screamed, George."

"I was watching television and really wasn't paying any attention to any sounds coming from outside. Of course, when she screamed, that got my attention fast."

"Just out of curiosity, do you know who the girl was?"

"No. Never saw her before. I assume it was probably some student from the college."

"Classes don't start at the college for another two weeks, so she must have been a local girl," I reasoned.

"Not necessarily. I've lived in this town for a long time. I've seen students come early just so they could get an apartment close to campus."

"Would you mind if I looked around a little, George?"

"No, I guess not. Are you a new cop or something? I thought I knew all the officers on our police force."

"No. I'm not a cop. I'm a professor at the college. It just would have been very easy for the police to have missed something in the dark last night. They probably didn't, but a second look can't hurt anything."

"Go ahead and have a look. My breakfast should be done by now anyhow."

"Thank you, and have a good day, George."

"You, too, Professor."

I started looking at the ground and under the hedge, starting at the driveway. George kept the grass trimmed along the hedge. I found several spots where the dirt just under the hedge had been disturbed like a foot had kicked it. I figured the girl had done that while struggling when she was being dragged behind the hedge. Then at the corner where the girl and her attacker had been on the ground, I spotted a small round object under the hedge. I picked it up and examined it.

It was about the size of a medium-sized button, flat with a strange design on it, gold with a black background. It looked to me like an oriental design. I turned it over. On the back side was a small ring, which a person could use to sew it onto something.

I looked at my watch. With a start, I realized I was a little late picking up Denise. I slipped the object into my pocket and raced back to my house. I locked the house door, jumped into my car, and sped off down the street. I caught Denise a block from her house, walking. I stopped. Then leaning across the seat, I pushed the car's passenger door open.

I briefly explained what happened the previous evening. She had a bit of a shocked look on her face as I told her about the attack.

"My God! When are the police going to catch this pervert? Do you know if the girl is very badly hurt?"

"She didn't seem to be physically hurt when I held her until the paramedics got there. But I really don't know for sure. I have something I would like you to look at before I turn it over to the police." I reached into my pocket and produced the object I had picked up from under the hedge. I placed it in her hand. She examined the piece closely. "The design looks oriental to me. Do you recognize the design, or do you think it's just something very common?" I asked.

"I don't know, John," she said slowly. "A lot of times, I will surf the internet in the evening when Mom is busy, or I just don't have anything else to do. It seems like I've seen this design, or one very similar to it, on the internet not that long ago. I don't remember for sure right now. I'll do a little exploring and see what I can come up with."

"That would be great. Since it wasn't dirty, I'm pretty certain it must have come off the girl or her attacker. If it did come from one of them, it would probably be important to know which one it came from."

"Why don't we go up to the hospital later this afternoon? We could check and see how that girl is getting along and ask her if she recognizes this at the same time," Denise suggested.

"That is a good idea. Are you good at drawing?"

"Pretty good. Why?" she asked.

"Since I can't draw a straight line with a ruler, why don't you make a drawing of this so we have a copy to work with, because I have to go down to the police station and make a statement for the sheriff and drop this off after we're done at the hospital. I don't want the sheriff to be able to say I withheld evidence if this thing turns out to be just that— evidence."

"Sure, John. I'll make a drawing of it this afternoon sometime. What time do you want to go to the hospital?" she asked as she got out of the car in front of the Music Building.

"How about three o'clock?"

"That will be fine. See you later."

I left the Music Building and drove to my classroom building. My eyes fell on the observatory when I pulled up in front of the classroom building. I had been itching to get a look at that telescope ever since I laid eyes on the observatory that first time. Now was a good time to do just that. I drove on up to the observatory and parked in a white-rock parking area. I got out of the car and walked toward the observatory door with great anticipation. I pulled the key out of my pocket and promptly dropped it. As I was picking the key up, I noticed something lying half covered up among the white rock. I picked it up with the key.

I turned it over in my hand. It was gold in color. It wasn't all scratched up, so it couldn't have been here too terribly long, even though I didn't think there had been too many people around the observatory lately. After examining it, I decided it had to be a money clip, particularly since it had the initials FD engraved on it.

"Can I help you with something?" a woman's cold voice asked from behind me, startling me. I spun around to face the owner of the voice.

A tall stately middle-aged stately woman with a no-nonsense air about her and dressed in a severe but fashionable skirt suit and high-heeled shoes stood before me.

"I don't think so, ma'am. I was about to go into the observatory."

"Are you aware that the observatory is kept locked at all times?"

"I know. It's a good thing I have a key."

"Then you must be the new professor of astronomy?"

"Yes, ma'am. Professor John Brennon at your service."

"Professor Brennon, I'm very happy to meet you. I'm Florence Duncan."

"The granddaughter—" I started to say.

"The great-granddaughter," she said, interrupting me, "of the founder of this college. I'm the one who had the new telescope installed. I also made it possible for your new department to be formed."

"I am very happy about all that, Miss Duncan. If you would care to join me, I thought I would take a peek at what we have here."

I slipped the gold money clip into my pocket. The key inserted into the lock with a little difficulty, probably because I doubted if the lock was turned all that often. I got it unlocked and pulled the steel door open, allowing a shaft of light to partly illuminate the observatory's dark interior. I started to enter.

"Maybe I had better go in first," Florence said quickly. "I know where all the light switches are."

I stepped back, allowing her to enter first. She entered, disappeared for a second, and then the lights came on. I then stepped into the observatory.

The big sophisticated, modern telescope took up most of the room inside the observatory. Along one wall was a bank of computers, monitors, and controls above and on a shelf- type work area that operates the telescope. I slowly walked down the row of instruments, quickly scanning them, while Florence wandered on her own. I found the control for the dome's slit. The slit started to rumble open when I turned the control knob to "Open." Sunlight flooded into every corner of the observatory. I stopped the slit when it was a fourth of the way open. Florence came and stood beside me.

"Well, Professor, what do you think of the equipment I had installed?"

"From what I can see, everything looks to be of excellent caliber. It will be a pleasure to work with such excellent equipment."

"I'm looking forward to seeing some spectacular pictures out of this telescope. I must be going now, though, because of other obligations," she said, heading for the open door.

"Before you go, Miss Duncan, I have one question I need to ask."

"Yes. What is it?" she asked, turning around to face me.

"I've been told the telescope hasn't had regular maintenance since it was installed. Is that true?"

"It's been maintained. I had contracted with the telescope manufacturer to do regular maintenance on it until the college hired a professor. Now that the college has done that, its maintenance will be your responsibility. However way you want to do it or whomever you hire to do it will be fine with the college. Now I really do have to go."

She turned back to the door and quickly left. I went to the door and stood there for several seconds, watching her walk rapidly toward her mansion.

The rest of the day, until it was about time to pick up Denise, I spent familiarizing myself with the telescope's controls. All too soon, it was time to go. I closed the top and carefully locked the door. Denise was waiting outside the Music Building when I pulled up. She slid into the Caddy.

"So what did you do all day?" she cheerfully asked.

"I spent the day in the observatory, familiarizing myself with it. I also met our illustrious Florence Duncan today. And I found a gold money clip. Unfortunately, there wasn't any money in it."

"How did you meet Duncan?"

"I was ready to go into the observatory when she basically appeared out of nowhere. We talked for a minute outside. Then we went inside. She stuck around for a few minutes, then she left. That left the rest of the day for me to explore the observatory by myself. It was great!" Denise laughed at my enthusiasm.

"I'm glad you enjoyed yourself today, John. Do you know where the hospital is?" she asked.

"I think so. When I've had time, I've been studying the city map I had gotten from the college when I first arrived."

We arrived at the hospital, parked the car, and went in. "Can I help you, folks?" a pretty young girl asked, smiling from behind the information counter.

"I think so. Last night, a young lady was brought in who had been attacked. We don't know the girl's name, but we would like to just see how she is getting along."

"I can help you with that. Let me check and see what room she is in." She pulled the information up on her computer. "Miss Joyce Collins. Room 312. That would be on the third floor."

"Thank you," I said.

"You're welcome."

Denise and I took the elevator up to the third floor. We had no trouble finding Room 312. A frail-looking girl lay in a white- sheeted hospital bed. Her eyes were closed when we entered the room but fluttered open as Denise moved to one side of her bed and I moved to the other side. Fear sprang into the girl's eyes when she saw we were somebody other than hospital personnel.

"It's okay, Miss Collins. Don't be frightened," I said quickly. "I'm the guy that chased your attacker away last night. This is a friend of mine, Denise Cole. How are you feeling?"

"I'll be okay, thanks to you. I have a couple of cracked ribs. You stopped him from doing anything worse. Thank you."

"I'm glad I was there to stop him. I would like you to look at something, if you would." I took the button out of my pocket and handed it to Joyce. "I found this under the hedge where your attacker had you down on the ground. Is it something that came off a piece of your clothing that you were wearing last night?"

"No. I don't have any clothing with buttons like that. Sorry," she said after looking it over carefully.

"That's okay. Don't worry about it. You just relax and take it easy. My friend and I hope you get to feeling better fast. We'll check and see how you are getting along in a couple of days."

Joyce closed her eyes then. Denise and I eased ourselves out of the room. Our next stop was the police station.

The police station was a two-story structure. I had heard someone mention that the jail cells were on the second floor with the first floor devoted to offices, interrogation rooms, and the booking area. There was plenty of activity, but no chaos among the half dozen officers in the room. The room was well lighted without being harsh. A fairly large bulletin board was partly filled with wanted posters. The rest of the board was devoted to fliers of missing people.

"Can I help you, sir?" an officer behind a counter asked.

"Yes. I'm John Brennon. The sheriff wanted me to come in and give a statement about last night."

"The sheriff has been expecting you. Go on into his office."

Denise and I went through a swinging gate and headed for a door that had "Sheriff" stenciled on it. I knocked and was told to enter. We entered an orderly office that was furnished with a desk and two chairs.

"I was wondering if you were going to make it in today, Professor, considering the time of day it's getting to be."

"I apologize, Sheriff. It's been a busy day."

"I understand. Give your statement into this recorder, and then someone will type it up for you to sign—after you read it over for accuracy, of course."

I gave my statement, and an officer came in and took the recorder out into the other room to transcribe my statement.

"I have something to show you, Sheriff," I said, taking the button out of my pocket and laying it down on the desk in front of the sheriff. "I found this under the bushes where the girl was attacked last night. We stopped at the hospital and showed it to the girl. She didn't recognize it. I figure it must have come from the attacker."

"Professor, buttons like this are a dime a dozen. I don't see where this is going to help at all. What were you doing at the crime scene this morning?" he asked somewhat belligerently.

"I live three houses down the street, remember? I went for a walk this morning. The owner of the property where it happened happen to be out in the yard, so I stopped to talk with him. While I was there, I took a quick look around and found this under the bushes."

"I appreciate your interest and bringing in what you thought was a piece of evidence, but remember, this is a police matter, not something for an amateur to be meddling in."

"And if I should happen to come across some information or other evidence, shall I just let it lay?" I asked angrily.

"No, of course not. All I'm saying is that this person has killed once, twice, counting the dog, already. The last thing I need is to have an innocent person's death on my conscience. Just let the police do its job. We will get the person responsible. That is a promise."

Just then, an officer brought in a typed copy of my statement. I carefully read the statement to make sure of its accuracy, then signed it. I handed it to the sheriff.

"Okay, Sheriff. I have to be going now. I hope you do catch the guy soon." Denise and I got up and left the police station.

"I meant to ask if you were able to get a drawing done of that button we just left in there?" I asked Denise.

"Sure did."

"Good. I would still like you to do a little exploring on the web if you have time and don't mind."

"No problem, John. By the way, the garage called and said they would have my car done by tomorrow afternoon. Would you be able to take me down to the garage around three o'clock?"

"I'll be happy to. I'm going to miss our morning and afternoon conversations, though."

"We'll still see each other around campus. Plus, you are always welcome at my house. In other words, don't make a stranger of yourself. Okay?"

"Yes, ma'am," I said with a big smile.

The next morning, I picked Denise up as usual.

"Good morning, John. I surfed the web last night. I think I found what we are looking for. But you are not going to believe this. I have a little trouble believing it myself."

"Tell me, Denise," I implored. "Don't keep me in suspense."

"Okay, here it goes. You know I told you I thought I had seen that design on the web before? Well, I had. To begin with, you know what Satanism is, don't you?"

"Yes. It's the worship of Satan."

"Right. Well, I wasn't aware of how it has spread across the country like it has. You know how motorcycle gangs, like the Hell's Angels, has chapters in different parts of the country, right? Well, this group of Satanists has covens all over the country. The really interesting part of this whole deal, at least to me, is that they use that button, or whatever it is, for one form of identification between the members of the different covens."

"This doesn't make much sense to me, Denise. Why would they put all that information on the internet? To my way of thinking, they would want to keep their activities secret."

"I agree with you, John, but there are a lot of things on the internet a person wouldn't believe would be on it. For instance, child pornography is against the law, and people are arrested all the time for it, but it's relatively easy to find on the web. What I think is that someone put the information on the web in the hopes of drawing in new members. The top people may not even know it's on the web yet, or if they do, they might have decided to leave it on and see what happens."

"I'm not that computer literate, but I would imagine this information could be taken off the web as quickly and easily as it was put on."

"Yes, but the damage would have already been done as far as people seeing it who the head person wouldn't have wanted to see it."

"So what do we do now? How do we uncover the local coven, if there is one, without putting ourselves in serious danger?"

"I don't know, John. All I can say is, we'll have to keep our eyes and ears open. Maybe we can each give it some thought during the day today," she said as she got out of the car.

THREE

I left the Music Building and stopped at the Maintenance Building to check on the status of my classroom supplies I had ordered. They said some of the supplies had come in. I loaded what they had into my car and headed for my classroom.

I carried the supplies in, which consisted of a model of the moon, several astrological charts, and a couple of posters. I put the posters up on the walls and hung the charts above the blackboards. I started thinking about what Denise had said earlier.

One thing we could do was check copies of past newspapers at the library for any stories of bloody crimes or happenings in or around Cedar Falls. If there was anything in the papers, then we could talk with some of the town's old-timers.

I grabbed a bite at noon, then went back to working in the classroom until it was about time to pick Denise up. At a quarter to three, I locked up and got in my car. Denise trotted out of the Music Building when I pulled up. It was a nice day, so I had the top down on the car.

"Hello, my fine-feathered friend," she said cheerfully as she seated herself in the car. "Boy, will I be happy to get my car back, not that I haven't enjoyed going back and forth with you, John," she said quickly. "I have, but without my car, I feel I've lost a little bit of my freedom. Do you know what I mean?"

"Yes, I do, Denise. I feel that same way if my car is in the garage for any length of time. I also think I've figured out a way we could check out this occult thing."

"Okay. How is that?"

"One thing you need to keep in mind, Denise, is that this could get dangerous. Anybody who gets involved in this kind of thing plays for keeps."

"John, I have a curiosity streak in me a mile wide and just about as long. I certainly don't want to get hurt or dead, but if we are careful, neither one of them things will happen. If we get something concrete, we will take it to the police right away. Besides, the police certainly doesn't seem to be making much progress. And I don't see where this maniac has any intentions of stopping on his own. So what do you have in mind for us to do?"

"Okay. You win. What I have in mind is to check all the copies of the local paper's back issues for any stories of anything that would even smell of occult activities. We could go back ten or fifteen years. That should be far enough back. If there are any stories, we might be able to pick out a clue that might have been missed then."

"I'll tell you what, John. I eat between five and five thirty. Why don't I meet you at the library at six thirty? Do you know where it is?"

"I'll check it out on the town map. You know, whoever designed the town map was really smart when they wrote the names of most of the businesses and main buildings on it."

"Yes, they were."

I pulled up in front of the garage, letting Denise out. I waited for her to go in and come back out. She was in for about twenty minutes before coming out. She waved at me as she walked to her car. I stayed until she got in her car, backed out of the parking spot, and pulled out into the street. I left then to grab a bite to eat myself.

At six thirty, I was parked in front of the library. Denise showed up wearing a turtleneck sweater, blue jeans, and loafers. She was all ready for a couple hours of work. She was the picture of the pretty girl next door. We went on into the library.

"Hello, Denise," the librarian said softly. "How have you been? It's been a while since I've seen you."

"Hi, Judy. I know it's been a while since I've been in the library or that we have seen each other, and I apologize, but lately I've been real busy. Right now I'm getting ready for this coming semester. By the way, I would like you to meet John Brennon, a new professor at the college."

"Glad to meet you, John," Judy said, extending her hand. "Same here, Judy," I responded by shaking her hand. "What we need is the back issues of the *Cedar Falls Globe* for the last fourteen years."

"Okay. All our back issues are on microfilm. Follow me, and I will get the microfilm you want. Do either one of you know how to run a microfilm projector?"

"I do," I said.

"So do I," Denise said.

"Good. Follow me to where the machines are."

We followed Judy to the microfilm department. Denise and I split the reels of microfilm, so I had from seven years ago to the present. Denise took the reels from fourteen years ago to seven years ago. We sat down at two machines that were side by side. We threaded the film into our machines and started our search.

The Globe wasn't the size of a big metropolitan newspaper, but it did have ten pages per issue. We had worked for about an hour when I found something of interest. I had Denise take a look at the article with me.

The date of the issue was six years ago. It was reported that a fire had been spotted in a wooded depression on a farmer's private property. A car passing by on the road had seen the glow of the flames in the night and had called the Cedar Falls' fire department. By the time the fire department got on the scene, there was nobody around, just a fairly large fire burning. After the fire department extinguished the flame, the burnt remains of a dog about the size of a German shepherd was discovered among the ashes. The police found dog tags belonging to the dog of Florence Duncan among the remains of the burnt dog in the ashes. When asked about her dog, Miss Duncan said her dog had disappeared earlier in the day of the night of the fire. Since the dog was getting old, Miss Duncan theorized that the dog had just wandered off to die.

"I don't know about you, Denise, but that fire sure has the smell to high heavens of occult to me."

"It does to me too. If it wasn't for the dog, which to me has the ring of a sacrifice, I would say someone or a group started a fire. It got away from them, and when they heard the police and fire engine sirens, they split. But that dog in the fire changes the whole complexion of the event."

"That is my thought exactly," I said. "Let's see if there is anything more about this in later issues."

A story three days later, buried on page 7 of the paper, proclaimed the police as saying they believed the fire of three days earlier was caused by careless teenagers who were messing around and things got out of hand. No suspects was arrested. There was no mention made of the dog in this article.

Denise and I split the remaining six years of microfilm. By the time the library was closing, we had skimmed through the rest of the back issues without any success. We put all the microfilm reels back where they belonged. We went out to the checkout counter to say goodbye to Judy.

"Did you two find what you were looking for?" Judy asked. "I don't know. We did find the story on that fire on some farmer's property of six years ago. I wish I could talk to someone who was still in high school six years ago," Denise responded.

"Why?" Judy asked.

"Aspects of that fire interests me. The police said they never found out who started that fire. They just put it down to careless teenagers. If that was the case, there probably would have been some scuttlebutt about it among the high school kids. Especially where no serious damage had been done, kids tend to talk about their exploits."

"Well, my younger sister was a junior in high school six years ago. She now lives in Scootsdale, about thirty miles from here. We see each other pretty often. I was thinking of going to see her this weekend. I could ask her if she remembers the incident and, if she does, if she remembers any rumors or other talk that might have floated around school. She may or may not remember after six years."

"Thanks, Judy. I owe you one," Denise said.

"Let's get together next week one day for lunch." Judy said.

"I'd love to, Judy, but I just will not have time next week. First week of classes and all. We'll get together the following week. Classes will have started by then, and I will have my routine established. You can tell me then what, if anything, your sister remembered about that fire when she was in school. Okay?"

"Sounds good, Denise. Give me a call, and let me know what day. In the meantime, take care."

"You too, Judy. Talk to you later."

Denise and I left the library. We decided we would go have a cup of coffee before calling it a night. She jumped into my car, and we went to a restaurant that I hadn't been in yet.

"Do you think Judy's sister is going to remember anything she heard in her high school days after six years?" I asked Denise after we had gotten set down and we had our coffee.

"I don't know, John. I hope so, but there are times I have a hard time remembering something from a month ago, let alone six years ago. Are you ready for classes to start next week?"

"As ready as I'll ever be, I guess. I have most of my supplies. I have my lesson plans ready. What exactly do you teach in your classes?"

"Freshmen, I start teaching them how to read music. My part of the music curriculum is the singing part of it. Teaching kids how to play instruments isn't my thing. I teach the kids first to listen to themselves when they sing, then to listen to the people they are singing with. By the time they are seniors, I am teaching them how to respond to what a conductor is telling them what he or she wants them to do with his or her arm movements. By the time a student graduates, the student can usually conduct an orchestra themselves. I can play a piano and organ. I guess you could say I do the whole gamut, short of playing a lot of different instruments."

"I would really like to hear you play sometime. Are you ready to go?"

"Yes, I am."

"Okay. I'll run you back to your car then."

I dropped Denise off at her car back at the library. We said good night. Then she went her way, and I went my way. I reflected on how much my friendship with Denise had progressed in the short time since we had met. I found her to be very comfortable to be around. My feelings for her was deepening on a friendship level but not on a romantic level.

The next few days I spent between the classroom and observatory. By Sunday, the classroom was ready for the onslaught of students on Monday. The dormitories had filled up, and the town was awash with this semester's crop of students. I did notice that with all the new students on campus, only a few had gone up to the observatory, and I had never seen anybody try to go near the Duncan mansion. Of course, the high iron fence would keep all but the most hardy or athletic souls out of the mansion's grounds. The weather forecast had called for a crystal-clear night on Sunday. I decided Sunday evening I was going to open the top of the observatory and get myself some experience operating the telescope before trying to explain how to operate it to the students.

It was dusk when I parked my car by the observatory and got out. I glanced toward the Duncan mansion as I started to walk toward the observatory. I stopped and looked more intently. Since it was dusk, I couldn't be sure of what I thought I had seen. From where I was standing, it looked like a person fugitively moving around the outside of the mansion.

I was not a hero, but if Miss Duncan was up there in the mansion by herself and I had no reason to believe otherwise, she needed to be warned about a possible prowler. I grabbed a flashlight out of my car and proceeded toward the mansion. I got to the iron fence surrounding the property. I had no trouble going up and over it. In the deepening dusk, I was having a hard time keeping track of the prowler. I would spot the figure, then lose them, then spot them again. Finally, I got close enough that I could smell the smoke from a cigarette they were smoking. I snapped the flashlight on quickly, focusing the beam on the person's face.

The beam revealed a somewhat handsome face of a startled man I guessed to be in his midthirties. He was a big muscular man, two hundred pounds, and six feet, three inches tall. In the very brief inspection of his clothes as I swept my flashlight beam over him, he appeared to be fashionably dressed in what I perceived to be a tailored suit with no tie.

"Get that damn light out of my eyes," he ordered sternly.

"Not so fast, mister," I said, holding the beam steady in his face. "What are you doing up here?"

"Are you a cop or college security?"

"Neither, but that doesn't answer my question. Again, what are you doing up here?"

"I was taking a walk. What business is it of yours why I'm here? You don't own this house, I'm sure."

"Maybe I feel it's my civic duty to interfere when I see something that doesn't look right. Now it really doesn't matter to me if you answer me or not. You can always tell the police what you were doing on private property."

"And who is going to keep me here until the police get here? You?"

"If need be," I answered in a calm, steady voice.

He took a swing at my jaw. I saw it coming. I ducked the swing and followed with a punch into his midsection. He gave a grunt and bent forward. I followed that with an uppercut to his chin. The guy went down on his back and groaned. I picked up the flashlight and put its beam back on his face.

"Now stay put while I have the owner call the police. Maybe you didn't realize it, but this is private property, so it will be up to her if you're arrested or not."

"Yes, I know it's private property. It's my sister's private property," he said with a smirk in his voice.

"Your…your sister's?" I stammered, caught totally by surprise.

"Yes. Sister. My name is Frank Duncan. And would you mind telling me who you are?"

"John Brennon. Professor John Brennon, professor of Astronomy." I offered him my hand to help him up. He took it.

"Shall we go in? You can say hello to Florence," Frank suggested. Still in a state of surprise, I followed Frank into the mansion.

"We have a visitor, Florence," he called out as he closed the front door behind me. Florence came into the foyer from another room.

"Professor Brennon, to what do we owe the pleasure of your visit this evening?"

"Well, ma'am, I guess the long and the short of it is, I had come up to warn you that you had a prowler outside—"

"That would be me," Frank said, interrupting me.

"So you could call the police," I finished. "I didn't know if you were alone or not. That is when I ran into your brother outside, and since I had no idea who he was, I had no choice but to confront him and ended up knocking him down. I apologize to both of you, if either one of you feel I stuck my nose into your business."

"On the contrary, Professor Brennon," Florence said, reaching out for my hand, "I am in your debt for caring enough about my safety to put your own safety at risk. Thank you."

"I haven't been in town all that length of time, which is why I had no idea that you had a brother, Miss Duncan."

"Let's just say Frank comes and goes all the time. He may be here for days or months at a time, and then he's gone for days or months at a time. I'm sure a lot of people in town isn't even aware I have a brother."

"Well, I had better be on my way. Good to have met you, sir. I'm sorry it couldn't have been under different circumstances," I said, offering him my hand.

He took it in a firm grasp and shook it. "Don't give it a thought. This wasn't the first time I've been hit. You have a good evening."

I took my leave and stepped out of the door. I stuck my hands in my pockets as I walked down toward the street that circled up in front of the mansion. My fingers touched the money clip I had been carrying around since I found it. I remembered the initials on the clip as FD. FD could very easily translate into Frank Duncan. Since I was already here and he was here, it wouldn't hurt to ask him if the clip was his. I stopped, turned around, and walked back to the front door. Just as I was about to knock, I noticed the door was slightly ajar. I thought I had pulled the door clear shut behind me when I left, but apparently, I hadn't. I started to step inside and announce my presence, but the angry voices of Frank and Florence Duncan stopped me.

"When are you going to leave, Frank?" she demanded to know.

"What's the hurry, sis? I've only been here for a month or two. And I've been keeping pretty much out of sight like you asked.

"Yes, you have laid low, but it seems things have a tendency to happen when you are around. Life would be so much easier if you led your life someplace separate from mine."

"A lot of your problem, sis, is that you worry too much. You need to relax. Do what you want to do, and to hell with what everybody else thinks. What good is it to have our kind of money if we can't do what we want when we want to do it?"

"Frank, to begin with, you're talking about *my* money, not our money. I work hard to earn it. I just allow you to spend some of it. Secondly, while you don't seem to worry about your reputation or what people think of you, I do think about my reputation, and I will do whatever it takes to safeguard it."

"Okay. Okay. Don't get hot under the collar," he chided her. "It's about time to go someplace with a little more life anyhow. This hick town is so boring. I will give it some thought about when I'll take off and where I'll take off to. Does that make you feel better?"

"A little. I'll feel better when you are gone again. The main thing I ask is that as long as you are here, try to stay out of trouble."

"Have I been in any trouble since I've been back this time, sister dear?" he asked sarcastically.

"Don't be a smart-ass. It doesn't become you. Just disappear as soon as you can."

I very carefully stepped away from the front door so as not to make any noise. I couldn't help but wonder what kind of trouble Florence and Frank had been referring to. He had said he had stayed out of trouble this time. I would take that to mean there had been other times when he was in town that he hadn't stayed out of trouble. Because Florence was such a proud person, I was sure she kept a tight rein on Frank so he wouldn't do anything really foolish. But my curiosity was aroused now. I had to find out what Frank had been up to in the past. I also decided to keep the money clip awhile longer.

Arriving back at the observatory, I unlocked the steel door. Rubbing my hands together with anticipation, I surveyed the now-lighted interior. I went to the control panel and turned the switch for the ceiling strip to open. The strip slowly started to rumble open, revealing a black star-studded evening sky. After turning some of the monitors on, I decided what part of the sky I wanted to look at. The telescope slowly moved into position to match the coordinates I had entered into the controls. The rest of the evening I spent lost in space, my mind wandering the black recesses of distant patches of the wonder-filled outer space.

Monday morning, I puttered around in my classroom, listening to the sounds of students out in the hall noisily making their way to the different classrooms. With every student, my class assembled itself. When the final bell rang, I had fifteen students seated, ready to explore the universe. Not a bad number for a new course at the start of a new year. I introduced myself and gave the class an overall picture of what we would be studying. I told them what books they would need for the course and which ones they would be able to buy at the college bookstore.

The first week went by pretty fast. I got my routine established and even learned to recognize a few of my students on sight.

That Friday afternoon toward evening, I decided to stop at Denise's house and see how she had made out after the first week of school. She and her mother were sitting on the porch when I pulled up in front of her house.

"Hello, John," Denise said gaily as she came out to the car to meet me. "Well, how did your first week go? Any future Galileos?" she asked.

"I probably have as many Galileos in my class as you have Mozarts in your class."

"That means you are very likely batting zero then. Come, have a seat. It's good to see you again."

"I wanted to get over to see you sooner, but I just couldn't seem to find the time. Tonight I just decided I was going to make the time. And I'm very happy to see you again, Mrs. Cole."

"It's a pleasure to see you again, John, and just call me Martha."

"Your wish is my command, Martha. And if there is ever anything I can ever do for you, just let me know."

"You never know, John. I just might take you up on that offer sometime."

"Anytime, Martha. Were you able to have that lunch with Judy this week?" I asked Denise.

"Yes, as a matter of fact, we had lunch together today. Her sister didn't remember too much. She did remember when that fire incident took place. This is a small enough town that kids and adults alike were talking about it at the time. She said rumor had it at the time that there was a secret group in town that dabbled in occult rituals. Nobody knew then who was on the membership roster. There was some speculation about this or that person but never any admission of membership or proof of such. The one thing there was never any speculation on was who the high priest was. It seemed the high priest was an older man. Rumor had it that he had a wide mean streak and the other members of the group wasn't about to do anything to bring his wrath down on their heads. Consequently, the identity of the high priest was never discovered. After that fire, rumors really flew for a while. But eventually, things died down, and the stories of this group kind of faded away."

"Were there any rapes or murders during that time?"

"Judy's sister didn't say anything to Judy about there being any rapes or murders in town then."

"What about between six years ago and this last rash of rapes?"

"Mom and I have only been here for three years, and until the rapes of the last couple of months, it has been a fairly quiet town."

"There was that one rape case a year or two ago, dear. The police never did solve that case either," Martha injected.

"You're right, Mom. I forgot about that incident."

"Did either one of you know that Florence Duncan has a brother?" I asked, looking from one to the other.

"No, I didn't know," Denise said. Her mother shook her head no also. "How did you find out?" Denise asked.

"You might have a hard time believing it, but I had to deck him last Sunday night."

"You decked him?" Denise asked with curiosity and a tinge of disbelief in her voice.

"Yep," I said, warming up to the telling of what happened. "I can make a long story short, or if you like, I could tell the long version with all the bells and whistles."

"That's fine," Denise said with a laugh. "We'll take the short version."

"You take all the fun out of telling a story, but okay, here it goes. I went up to the observatory Sunday evening. I noticed a figure moving around up by the mansion. It was dusk, so I couldn't get a real good look at them. This person looked too big to be Florence, so I hot-footed it up to the mansion to warn her of a possible prowler on her property, but the figure was too close to the front door for me to get past them. He was real belligerent, threw a punch, and missed, but mine landed. Then he told me his name and who his sister is. We went in. I explained to Florence Duncan why I was up there, apologized to Frank for decking him, and then left. I went back, though, and overheard them arguing. She wanted him to leave because she said he's nothing but trouble. Makes me wonder what kind of trouble she was referring to."

"Yeah," Denise said thoughtfully. "It makes me wonder too."

"Here we go again," Martha said with resignation in her voice. "If there is a mystery lying around loose, Denise can't help but be like Nancy Drew. She will start sniffing around until she unravels it. It may take her a while, but 99.9 percent of the time, she comes up with the correct solution to the mystery once she sinks her teeth into it. It worries me at times that she might one day get into something that she can't get herself out of with her whole skin intact."

"Mom, you know I'm always careful. When things get too hot, I back off. So you really don't need to worry. Besides, nothing ever happens in this town with the exceptions of the last couple of months."

"Where did you live before coming here?" I asked.

"The Big Apple. New York City. Mom and I were very happy to get out of the large city and into a smaller town, even though lately it's been feeling like we're back in New York with all the rapes going on."

"So have you drawn any theories about the rapist?"

"Only that it must be someone local, that they are not deranged or crazy, and that they lead very sedate everyday lives blending into a normal lifestyle. And I think he will be a fairly intelligent person. He is smart enough not to make mistakes or leave very few, if any, clues."

"From what you said a minute ago, Martha, I assume Denise had solved a case or two back in New York before the police did."

"A couple. You know how the police are, though. If they can't figure the case out, they don't want anybody else to either. The Cedar Falls Police Department doesn't seem to think any differently."

"Ladies, have you eaten dinner yet?" I asked, standing.

"No," Denise said.

"Good. Could I have the privilege and honor of both of your presence for dinner this evening? Your choice of restaurant, of course."

"That really isn't necessary, John," Martha said somberly as if she thought I was being a wise guy.

"I'm sorry if I offended you somehow, Martha, but I really would like to take you and Denise to dinner."

"That's more like it. We would love to join you for dinner." I ushered them into the Caddy after they picked the restaurant and drove them to it. It had some class to it without being a gourmet restaurant. We had a good meal along with great conversation. All too soon, the evening was drawing to a close, and it was time to take Denise and her mother home.

"I'll be in after I talk to John for a minute," Denise said to Martha after they had gotten out of my car in front of their house. "Okay, dear. Good night, John, and thank you for a lovely dinner."

"The pleasure was all mine, Martha." Martha went on inside the house.

CHAPTER

FOUR

"Where do we go from here, John?" Denise asked.

"One, I think we need to find out what the trouble is or what it was that Frank Duncan was involved in. Two, we need to follow up on this occult thing, maybe look at high school yearbooks from six or seven years ago. And three, if we find somebody of interest in the yearbook, maybe I could have a low-key talk with them about the past. Hopefully, they still live in town. We will have to see where that leads us and go from there."

"I don't understand. You said if we find somebody of interest in the yearbook. All a yearbook is going to tell us is what sports a person participated in or what clubs they might have been a member of. There certainly wasn't any Satan's club in the school's activities."

"You are right about that. A lot of times, though, the yearbook also lists the person's hobbies. I realize this is a long shot, but what have we got to lose? Maybe a little time is all."

"Okay. Let's say we get lucky and are able to identify someone who might possible have been involved with this occult thing then, what possible connection could that have with the raping that is going on now?"

"I don't know about you, but anybody who would worship Satan would do anything else up to and including murder. Since there wasn't any rapes, with the one exception, between then and this recent rash of rapes, the guy might not have been in town during that period of time. But now he is back with a vengeance. We may not find anything, but I think it's worth a try."

"I'll have an hour free after lunch Monday. I could go to the high school then and see if I can lay my hands on the yearbooks from six and seven years ago. Sometimes the school will sell them to you if they have any back copies lying around."

"That would be great, Denise. Between the classroom and the observatory, I'm going to be busy all day Monday. Could you stop by the observatory? It's where I'll be all afternoon. Then you can let me know how you made out at the high school?"

"Sure, John. No problem."

"Okay. See you tomorrow. Good night, Denise."

"Good night, John."

Monday, following lunch, I was pointing out the telescope controls and introducing the class to the telescope's operation when Denise showed up. I excused myself and went over to her.

"Did you get lucky?" I asked softly.

"Sure did. I got a copy of both years we are interested in. When did you want to go through them?"

"How about you come over to my place about seven o'clock for a steak hot off the grill, a tossed salad, a baked potato, and a little wine to top it all off? Another one of my diverse talents is cooking."

"Sounds good. I'll be there. See you later."

The rest of the afternoon went by agonizingly slow. Finally, I was able to lock everything up and head home. By six thirty, I was tossing the salad, chilling the wine, and getting ready to put the steaks on the grill. The potatoes were already in the oven. Denise got there a little early, so I started the steaks. After a delicious meal, we cleared the table to get down to work on the yearbooks.

We took the oldest book first. As we studied each page, especially if it was a group picture, we looked for any small item that seemed out of place or anything that might give an indication of anyone in the pictures of having any degree of interest in anything remotely connected to occult-type things. We also checked out the sports the kids played, the clubs everybody pictured participated in, and as many hobbies of the different kids as possible.

"Do you really think we might find something? After all, nobody is going to advertise that they are occult members," Denise asked.

"You are absolutely right. They wouldn't," I agreed. "However, I've found that most people like to show their membership in clubs or other organizations some way. Only sometimes they have to do it in a low-key fashion. As far as finding anything, that remains to be seen. I hope we do."

We kept looking.

"What's this, John?" Denise asked, pointing to one of four boys in the picture. I mean, I know what it is. It's a button on the guy's jacket sleeve, and I could tell the button had a design to it, but I can't tell for sure what the design is. I thought maybe you could."

"No, I can't either, but it wouldn't hurt to look into this a little closer because this does look a bit familiar. I have a friend back in Texas that is a genus when it comes to photography. I have seen him take a really blurred photograph like this one and sharpen the image up to near-perfect clarity. We can cut this picture out of the book and fax it to him. I'll ask him if he can get a clear photo back to me as soon as possible."

"What's the name of the guy in the picture?" Denise asked.

"Ah, it looks like his name is Jack Finks," I said. "If we are lucky, he might still live in town. Depending on what we come up with on the photo, I might want to talk to him."

I grabbed the phone book and checked to see if a Jack Finks was listed. There was. I wrote his name and phone number down. While Denise was carefully cutting the picture out of the yearbook, I was writing a short note to send with the photo.

"Here you go," Denise said, handing me the photo.

"Thanks," I said. I faxed the photo and note to my friend.

"Let's pack it in for the evening, Denise. I figure I should get a reply in three to four days, depending on how busy he happens to be right now. We can't do too much until we get this clear picture back."

We went out on the veranda to soak up some of the evening's fragrances and sounds. In the dim light shining through the window by the side of Denise, I could see a look of puzzled concentration on her face.

"A penny for your thoughts," I offered softly.

"I was just thinking about this maniac that's on the loose. What kind of guy could really enjoy raping somebody, and what kind could actually kill another person or animal and not have it bother them? I know if I hit and kill, or even injure, an animal on the road, I'd feel terrible for several days. Am I just too soft, John?"

"No, not at all. You just have a very loving nature. There needs to be a lot more people in this old world with your sentiments. You have a very beautiful personality, and I hope you never change."

"I didn't really plan on changing, but there are times I get hurt very easily. But I guess that is neither here nor there. I could sit out here all night, but I had better get home and hit the sack. Tomorrow is another day."

I watched her walk out to her car. After she left, I went back to the veranda and sat down. Somebody had mowed their grass today, and the smell of that freshly cut grass was still in the air. It reminded me of my days on the farm when I was a young boy. After all this time, the smell of freshly cut alfalfa still lingered in my nose. After a short period of time, my head started nodding, so I locked up the house and hit the bed.

In the next few days, I got my students indoctrinated into the operation of the telescope. I figured another few classes and these kids would know what they were looking at when looking through the telescope. That would allow them to truly appreciate the wonders of the universe.

Then one afternoon, I came home to find that a fax had come in on my machine. It was the fax from my friend in Texas, along with a note, that I had been waiting for.

The note read: "Hello, old buddy. Here is that photo you wanted cleaned up. Don't tell me you are already mixed up in something up there. Of course, you are. Anytime you get tired of that Nebraska weather, come on back down here. All your Texas friends say hello, and we all miss you. Keep in touch."

I couldn't help but smile as I pictured him engrossed with his photography. We spent a lot of good times together camping, barhopping once in a while, and chasing girls. He had a slim build bordering on being skinny, was about six feet and four inches tall, was a compassionate friend to his friends, and has a very cheerful disposition. I would definitely have to keep in touch with him.

I looked at the clear picture in my hand and then compared it to the photo taken from the yearbook. The difference in clarity was astounding. The design on the button in the photo looked identical to that on the button I had picked up from under George's hedge. I would need to make a comparison between the photo and the drawing Denise had done. I called Denise's house, and Martha answered.

"Hi. Is Denise there, Martha?"

"No. Not right now. She had gone down to the grocery store to pick up a few things. She should be returning shortly. Shall I have her give you a call when she gets back?"

"I would really appreciate it if you would, Martha. Thank you."

Denise left the house to go down to the Safeway store. She was thinking about Jack Finks as she drove to the store. If John decided to talk to him, she hoped he would be very careful.

She got to the store, went in, got what she needed, and came back out to her car. After loading the groceries into the trunk, she slid behind the wheel and left the Safeway parking lot. She hummed softly as she drove down the street.

Suddenly a ski-masked face appeared in her rearview mirror. A wicked-looking gun was in the person's hand. He pressed the muzzle of the gun against Denise's neck.

"Pull into that alley right up there," he ordered her urgently. Denise drove into the designated alley. "Now you are going to deliver a message to Mr. John Brennon for me. He prevented me from enjoying myself with a girl not too long ago. I know about your exploits in New York City, and I know about your boyfriend's exploits in Texas. It doesn't matter how I know. I just do. You tell your boyfriend to mind his own business or I might have to take my pleasure with you if you both don't leave me alone. Wouldn't you like to have me visit you some night, honey?"

To let her know he meant business, he let one hand slide down to her breast. "No! No!" she cried, recoiling from his touch.

"Okay. You two back off then."

He pulled the gun away from her neck, but she could still see his face in the rearview mirror. Just as a strange odor became prevalent in the car, the masked stranger covered Denise's nose with a cloth. Denise's body went limp. The stranger took the cloth off her nose after ten seconds. He pulled the mask off his head and stuffed it into a baggy pants pocket. Then he exited her car, leaving her unconscious body slumped over in the front seat. He quickly moved down the alley and disappeared among other people on the sidewalk.

I waited a good half hour for Denise to return from the store. When she didn't call, I called her house again. Martha answered the phone again.

"John," she said with concern in her voice, "I'm beginning to worry about Denise. She said she was going straight to the store and then straight home. Even if they were busy in the store, she should have been back by now. This isn't like her to be late."

"Did she have her cell phone with her?"

"As far as I know, she did. She generally does. She would have called if she had any trouble, but she hasn't."

"Relax, Martha," I said soothingly. "Which store did she go to?"

"The Safeway store on Highway 2 going south out of town."

"Okay, Martha, you sit tight. I'm going to drive over to the store. Maybe she has car trouble or maybe a flat tire and she couldn't call you because her phone is dead. I'll check the parking lot, and if I don't see her car there, I'll check her most likely and direct route home. I'll give you my cell number, and if she gets home before I get there, give me a call."

I gave Martha my cell phone number and then left the house. I kept my eyes peeled for Denise's car all the way to the store. When I got there without spotting her car on the street, I carefully and methodically searched the parking lot, but with no success. I then started to cover the route to her house. I drove slowly, checking to see if her car was parked anyplace on the street. Then I saw a car that was the same color as Denise's parked behind a building with just its back sticking out. I turned around in a driveway and drove back to the alley that separated the two buildings. I drove into the alley and stopped by the back of the car parked in back of the building. I got out of my car and looked around quickly. I started calling Denise's name as I cautiously approached the vehicle. I got to the driver's side window and found Denise unconscious. I yanked open the car door and gently shook her by her shoulders.

"Denise! Can you hear me?"

"Yes…yes, I can hear you," she answered slowly. She gently shook her head to help clear it.

"What in the world happened?" I asked.

"I came out of Safeway and put the groceries in the trunk. I came around to the driver's door and got in. I started to drive home. I got this far, and the next thing I know, a guy pops up in the back seat. He made me pull into where we are now. He said if you and I didn't start minding our own business, he would pay me a visit one night for the purpose of having his pleasure with me. He then put a cloth over my nose, and I passed out."

"Are you hurt anyplace?"

"No. He said this was just a warning."

"I'm glad you're not hurt. Let me call your mother and let her know you're okay."

I called Martha and told her I had found Denise and that she was fine. I told her Denise and I were going to stop at the police station to report Denise's assault before going home. I assured her I would make sure Denise got home safe. I hung up and turned back to Denise.

"Obviously, you didn't look in the back seat before you got into the car, but then I guess most people don't. I know I never think to. Have you ever seen the guy around town before?"

"He had a ski mask on."

"That doesn't surprise me. We need to go down to the police station now and report this, okay?"

"Sure, John."

I followed Denise down to the station. We got out of our cars and went in. "Is Sheriff Blocker in?" I asked.

"No. He's left for the day. Can I help you?" the officer behind the counter offered.

"Is Officer Hollister in?" Denise quickly asked.

"Yes. Ben, someone to see you," the officer said to Ben, who was around the corner.

"Hello, Ben," Denise said when he came around to the counter. "I have an assault I would like to report."

"Come on back into an interrogation room, and I'll take your statement and write a report."

We followed Ben back into an interrogation room. Ben asked if either of us wanted coffee or something else to drink. We declined, so Ben sat down, and we got down to business. After Denise gave her statement, Ben asked pretty much the same questions I had asked her and got the same answers from her.

"I don't quite understand what the guy meant about you two minding your own business. Are the two of you mixed up in something the police needs to know about? Is there anything I can do to help you, Denise?"

"Not unless you could let John and me look at your case files on the latest crime wave of rapes and murders. All John and I have done is look into a couple of things."

"You know I can't let you look at confidential files. If you or John here has any information that has a bearing on this investigation and you don't tell the police, you could face criminal charges. Now what are them couple of things? Level with me, Denise. I don't want to see anything more happen to you."

"Right now we don't have anything concrete. When we do, we will be sure and let you know. I want it on the record that I was assaulted, though."

"I doubt if we can do much with the little bit you were able to give me. However, I will make some extra swings past your house for a while. And for God's sake, if this thing escalates any further, let me know right away, okay, Denise?"

"Sure, Ben," she said, smiling at him.

"Are you going to stop at the hospital after you leave here?"

"No. I'm fine. He didn't hit me or anything. I think he drugged me because he didn't want me to see what direction he took off in. I don't see what difference that would make, but apparently, he did. Either that or he might have taken his mask off before he was able to get too far away from the car. Well, if there is nothing else, Ben, we would like to be on our way."

"I'm done, Denise. Until we get this person responsible for all the present trouble locked up, I would recommend that you lock your car whenever you are out of it. Going into a store for just a minute or two gives somebody time to duck into the back seat. In other words, try to be as careful as you can be."

"Will do, Ben. And thank you."

We left the police station, and I walked her to her car.

"I don't know if you are aware of how much Ben really likes you, Denise," I said.

"I know how much he does. And I like him a lot, too, just not as much or in the same way. I've gone on a few dates with him, and he has always been the perfect gentleman. But the last thing I want to do is lead him on. Maybe one day my feelings could change, but not right now. Right now, I just want to get home and relax."

Martha was waiting outside the house, on the porch. As soon as Denise got out of her car and was halfway to the house, Martha met her. She gave Denise a hug and then held her at arm's length to get a good look at her.

"Are you sure you're not hurt, dear?" she asked apprehensively.

"I'm fine, Mom. A little shook up, but fine. Is it going to be long before dinner?"

"About an hour. You are going to stay for dinner, John," she informed me with finality.

"Sure. Thank you. I'd be happy to stay for dinner."

"I'm going to take a shower before dinner, Mom, since I have time to."

"Okay, dear."

"I'll bring the groceries in, Martha."

"Thank you, John. Just put them on the counter, and I'll put them away."

I grabbed Denise's car keys that she had laid beside her purse. I went out, got the groceries out of the trunk, and brought them into the kitchen. I then went back out and made sure Denise's car was locked up tight. I went back into the kitchen and checked to see if there was anything else I could help Martha with. She shooed me out of the kitchen and into the living room. I sat down in an overstuffed chair by the fireplace. I had just about dozed off when Denise came into the living room.

Her long black hair was damp from the shower. Her face was radiant with a fresh scrubbed softness to it. A cashmere sweater graced her slim torso, and a pair of figure- flattering slacks encased her legs. She stuck her head into the kitchen to see if Martha needed any help. Martha said no and sent her back into the living room to keep me company until dinner was ready. She came in and curled up on the sofa. "Now how did you happen to find me?" she asked.

"Well, I wanted to tell you I had gotten that fax back from my friend in Texas. I called the house here, and your Mom said you had gone to the store but was late getting back. I told her I would go looking for you. I checked the store parking lot first. When I didn't find your car there, I started to check your route or at least what I thought your route would be back to the house. That was when I saw the back of your car sticking out from the back of that building. I checked it out and found you."

"Even though the guy had already left, I am real glad you found me when you did."

"I'm just glad you didn't get seriously hurt. Do you by chance have that sketch you made of that button handy?"

"Sure. It's right here in my files."

While she got the sketch out of her files, I moved over to the couch so we could both examine the clear photo and sketch at the same time. She brought the sketch over and sat down beside me. After close examination, we came to the same conclusion. The designs were identical.

"I'm going to have a talk with this guy. Before you say anything about coming with me, I think I had better talk to this guy by myself. I'll fill you in on what I learn afterward."

Just then, Martha came into the living room and announced that dinner was ready. The table was laid out with a nice roast beef, mashed potatoes and gravy, a green-bean casserole, hot dinner rolls, and iced tea. It was a thoroughly delicious meal complemented by very pleasant dinner conversation. After the three of us relaxed on the porch for a little while, I decided it was time for me to leave.

"Are you going to talk to Finks tomorrow?" Denise asked me as I was leaving.

"I'm going to try to get in touch with him, maybe set something up with him for tomorrow afternoon or evening."

"You be careful, John. It seems the stakes have gotten higher if what happened this afternoon is any indication."

"I promise I'll be careful, Denise."

"Don't leave me out of it either," she pressed. "I still want you to keep me informed."

"After I talk to Jack, I'll give you a call or come over like I said I would. You are the one who needs to be careful. After all, it wasn't me they stopped, although I wish it had been me."

"Good night, John."

"Good night, Denise."

The next day, I had the afternoon free. I went home, grabbed a sandwich, and got the paper out that had Jack's name on it. I noticed I had written his phone number down but not his address. I got out the phone book, found his address, and wrote it down. I dialed his phone number. He answered on the fifth ring.

"Is this Jack Finks?" I asked.

"Yes. Who is this?"

"My name is John Brennon. I would like to meet with you someplace and talk about what I think could be a common interest."

"What interest could that possibly be?"

"Let's just say I saw a picture of you in your high school junior year yearbook. You had a jacket on. The sleeve button of that jacket is what really interests me."

"And why would that sleeve button interest you?" he asked cautiously.

"I've done a little research, Jack. You know, the internet is an amazing invention. If a person has reasonable intelligence, they can get most any information they want off the web. Take, for instance, that button."

"Before we go there, I think it might be a good idea if we sat down face to face. Could you come to my house?"

"I think so. When would you like for me to come over?"

"About three o'clock this afternoon. I have something I have to take care of first. I'll be home after three."

"Okay. I'll be there," I said and hung up.

I thought about if I should take any precautions before going over to Jack's. After the warning that was given to Denise, I knew I had to be careful, but I wasn't going to let myself become paranoid either. So I figured the best thing to do was to leave a message for Denise at the college that I was going to be at Jack's at three o'clock, along with his address.

At three o'clock, I pulled up in front of a large two- story white clapboard frame house bearing Jack's address. A Volkswagen about ten years old sat in the driveway. The yard wasn't overgrown, but it was ready for a mowing. I walked up to the door and knocked. After fifteen or twenty seconds, the inside door opened.

A slightly disheveled guy in his midtwenties stood there, waiting for me to identify myself. He was wearing a white T-shirt and faded blue jeans. His feet were shoeless.

"Hi. I'm John Brennon. May I come in?"

"Yeah, sure. Come in," he said, pushing the screen door open. I stepped inside, acutely aware of Jack closing the door behind me. The interior of the house was furnished in secondhand furniture. I didn't see anything in the room to indicate an interest in the occult.

"Have a seat," Jack offered. I sat down on the sofa. "You mentioned a jacket on the phone, or maybe I should say a button on that jacket. You also mentioned getting information off the internet on the phone. Exactly what information were you referring to?"

"Before I answer, would you tell me where you got that button that was on the sleeve of the jacket you had on when the group picture was taken for the yearbook?"

"I think I remember the jacket. But what would make you think the button was not the original button?"

"I think you know as well as I do the significance of that design on that button. I'd like to know where you got the button and from whom. Also, since you and I both know what that button was used for, why would you wear it for everybody to see?"

Jack looked at me for several seconds, and then he got up and started to pace about the room. Finally, he seemed to make up his mind, and he sat back down.

"Okay, I'll tell you all about it. First, I was never able to make it in sports in high school, but I wanted to belong or be part of something. When I learned about this coven in town through rumors, I checked into it. After I was accepted and the button was presented to me, I wanted to let everybody know that I had finally made it into something. Naturally, as soon as the high priest discovered that I had sewed the button onto the jacket, he ordered me to remove it immediately, which I did. I was young and foolish then. This coven only has six members in it now, plus the high priest. When I got into it back in high school, there was twice that number of members. The membership numbers has dropped off because the coven's activities have become so sporadic. A lot of the time, nobody knows if the high priest is even around because of some of the long intervals between meetings. I am seriously thinking of quitting the coven myself. Of course, if I do, I'll have to move and change my name. The high priest doesn't take kindly to anybody quitting because there is a chance the person quitting will talk to the wrong person, like I might be doing now."

"I promise I will not spread the word around town about this. Do the members of each coven know whom the other members of their own coven are?"

"Not unless you yourself deliberately reveal your identity to another member. The only reason you found out about me is because I wasn't thinking when I wore that particular jacket when I went to have that picture taken. Everybody has their face covered when they arrive at the rituals or meetings, during the rituals or meetings, and when we leave a ritual or meeting."

"Does anybody know who the high priest is?"

"Not that I know of."

"Have you seen that article on the internet about the button and its design?"

"Yes."

"Have you any idea who put that article on the web?"

"It could have been anyone, but nobody ever found out who for sure. All I know is, there was a whole lot of people who got very angry when the website came out."

"Do the covens still use that design and button as their recognition between members?"

"Yes."

"Thank you, Jack," I said, rising. "I hope everything works out for you."

I left then. Denise would still be at the college, so I figured I would stop by her house later or call her later to fill her in on my talk with Jack.

I went home and decided I needed to do some housework since I didn't have a maid service come in and do it. After I was done with what needed to be done, I threw a TV dinner in the microwave oven. The phone rang just as I was finishing the TV dinner.

"Hello."

"Hi. This is Denise. I kept waiting for you to call, but my curiosity wouldn't let me wait any longer. How did it go?"

"First, sorry I didn't call you sooner, but I had some things I had to do around the house. It went well with Jack. Once he realized I knew what I was talking about, he pretty well opened up."

"Do you think you learned anything that will help us?"

"I don't know, Denise. I learned the coven around here is still semi-active. It's membership is only half of what it was six, seven years ago. Everybody kept, and still keeps, their identities secret from each other, and nobody knew who the high priest was or is. There was one thing I found interesting. Jack was talking like he would like to quit the coven. Maybe over the course of time, he has become disillusioned with the whole occult thing. I hope so."

"That happens sometimes. Do you think this Jack character has any connection with the rapes and murders?"

"I really don't think so. Right now he isn't very high on my suspect list. He doesn't come across to me as the most savory person I've ever met, but I have trouble visualizing him as a rapist and killer. He did seem to be disheveled, though."

"Do you think he will be in danger if the occult's head honcho finds out he spilled his guts to you?"

"Possibly, but I hope not. Fundamentally, any Satan worshipping society is full of bloodlust. The sacrifices in the rituals demonstrate that. And I don't think they like it when members leave. Jack said if he left the coven, he would have to leave town, change his name, and disappear."

"So where does that leave us, John? Where do we go from here?"

"The way I see it, we will probably have to work our way up through the rank and file of members to find out who the high priest is. I think the rapist and killer will end up being one of the guys of the coven. I don't think any of the other members will make the same mistake Jack did with the button."

"So about all we can do is watch and wait for someone to surface?" she asked.

FIVE

"No. We both have classes to teach, I know. But I intend to follow Jack as much as I have time for when not teaching a class, correcting papers, or doing other things pertaining to my job. Even if none of the coven members turn out to be the rapist and killer, I would still love to see this coven broken up."

"That makes two of us. I could follow this Jack character some of the time too," she offered.

"I would rather you wouldn't, Denise. It could be too dangerous. Would Ben Hollister, the deputy, get police information for you if you asked him to?"

"He might—if I asked real sweetly and depending on the information I would be asking for."

"We can give it a try. If he will, you will be our mole inside the police department. I doubt very much if I could get any information from them at all. It could be a big help to us."

"Okay…I guess," she said with resignation in her voice. I could tell she didn't like the idea of not being in the thick of it, but her safety was utmost in my mind.

In the next four days, I managed to trail Jack several times. The last time I tailed him, he met with a man who was a stranger to me. They met at a cafe. They talked for about an hour, and then they left. I decided to follow the stranger. He drove to a fourplex apartment building. The area inside the front door where the mailboxes were located was very well lit. I watched as the guy moved up the stairs to the second floor. I dashed into the apartment building. I got the names of the upper apartment renters off the mailboxes. One name was that of a woman, but the other name was that of a man. I wrote the man's name down and left. I decided to stop at Denise's on my way home.

"Good evening, John," she called out to me from the porch as I got out of my car. "I'm glad you stopped by. I was beginning to feel neglected." She said this in a joking way.

"I've been busy, busy, busy, my dear girl. I might or might not have gotten lucky this afternoon. I followed Jack to a cafe where he talked with another guy for about an hour. I followed the other guy home and got his name. Amos Gains. Does the name ring any bells?"

"Nooo. I could have lunch with Ben tomorrow maybe. I could ask Ben if the name rings any bells with him. Can you stop by my office tomorrow afternoon sometime?"

"Sure. No problem."

We chatted for a while then just enjoyed the evening. Martha had gone to her normal Wednesday night bridge game, so Denise and I had the evening to ourselves. We talked about a variety of subjects, including crime and punishment.

"When this guy who has done all these rapes and murders is caught, what do you think his punishment should be?" she asked.

"Well, for rape, he needs to be surgically fixed so he could never get an erection again, plus prison time. For murder, I believe the penalty should be execution, and I mean no later than sixty days after the trial is over." I said.

"A lot of people say the state would be no better than the killer themselves if that state executed every person that was convicted of murder. Most of the same people say that by executing the murderer, it will not bring the victim back to life. That isn't my way of thinking. My thoughts run more in line with yours."

"And they are absolutely right. By executing the killer, it wouldn't bring the victim back to life. But by serving a life sentence, there is the possibility of either the prisoner escaping from prison or getting out on parole. Either way, innocent people are put at risk in case the killer strikes again. What do they have to lose? They already have a life sentence hanging over them when they are caught and sent back. I feel a dyed-in-the- wool killer wouldn't let anything stop them from killing again. So if they are executed, you can figure one or more innocent lives are saved. Well, that is my sermon for tonight, Denise. I had better head home and get ready for tomorrow."

"I'm glad you stopped by, John. I'll see if I can't set up that lunch date with Ben tomorrow. Good night."

"That was a real surprise when you called last night, Denise," Ben said as Denise and he sat down for lunch.

"Well, it's been a while since we've gotten together, but with the new semester starting, I have been extremely busy. I know good friends should stay in touch. So how have things been going for you?" Denise asked.

"Pretty good. Everybody has been working some overtime patrolling the streets. Our one detective has been putting a lot of extra time in on this rape-and-murder case."

"Has there been any real progress on it?"

"We have leads we are following up on. We have one guy we are closely investigating right now."

"His name wouldn't be Jack Finks, would it?" Denise asked.

"Yes, it is," Ben said, surprised. "Nobody but Detective Jerkins and a few other officers knew we had any interest in Finks. How do you know him, and what do you know about him?" Ben asked suspiciously.

"John and I ran across his name when we were looking some things up. Does the name Amos Gains ring any bells with you?"

"Kind of. The name does have a familiar ring to it."

"Do you think you could possible run his name through whatever you run a name through to check if they have a record?"

"Be honest with me, Denise. Is the only reason you had lunch with me today was to ask me for a favor?"

"No, Ben," she replied sincerely. "I honestly think you are a heck of a nice guy, and I like you very much as a friend. I hope we'll always be friends. I'm sorry, but at least right now, I just don't have romantic feelings for you. I hope you understand, and we can continue to have a good friendship."

"Sure, Denise. No more than a good friendship it shall be. I'll check on this Amos Gains and see what pops up."

"If you could give me a call at my office at the college when you find out anything one way or another, I would really appreciate it, Ben."

"I'll see if I can't run his name through today yet."

"Thank you. I promise we'll get together more often."

They finished their lunch with general chit-chat. Then Denise went back to the college, and Ben went back on duty. A couple of hours later, Ben called Denise.

"I had time to run Gains's name through the system. He does have a rap sheet. His most serious crime was assault and battery. His least serious offense was shoplifting. It looks like he started his criminal career back in his late teen years. What made you ask about Gains?"

"Gains and Finks had coffee together the other day. They were together for about an hour. Since I know a little bit about Finks, the two of them together made me wonder what Gains was all about."

"The police wasn't aware Finks and Gains knew each other. From what you're telling me, it would seem they are friends. I'll pass this new information on to Jerkins. Thanks, Denise."

"Thank you for running that through. Take care, and I'll talk to you later, Ben.

I stopped at the Music Building later that afternoon like I told Denise I would. It took me a little while to find her office, but I finally did. "Denise Cole, Professor of Music" was emblazoned on the door with brass letters. I knocked.

"Come in," Denise's voice said from the other side of the door. It was large enough not to be cramped. An antique desk, a four-drawer filing cabinet, a comfortable-looking office chair, and a couple of upholstered chairs took care of the office furniture. Books filled shelves that took up the wall at the back of the desk.

"And what do you think of my humble office, John?" she asked lightly.

"It's a nice office, Denise. I especially like this desk. Antique, isn't it?" I asked, running my hand over the smooth wood.

"Yes, it is. It was a gift from my mom when I graduated from college. It means a lot to me. I know it's a little big for this office, but ask me if I care. Have a seat. I did ask Ben about Gains. He has got a rap sheet from shoplifting to assault and battery from his teen years to the present."

"He sounds like a real beauty, even worse than Jack maybe. There are more and more unsavory characters running around here. But that is what happens when a person starts to scratch the underbelly of society."

"Isn't that the truth. Unfortunately, when you go after a rat, you need to look in the sewer where the rats are," she agreed.

"Well, thanks for the information on Gains. I'm going to be tied up this evening with a few of my students. Everything is just right for us to observe a certain constellation. They wanted some extra credit, so I told them to be at the observatory this evening."

"Have fun," Denise said as I left her office.

I got up to the observatory just as the sun was slipping below the horizon. The sky was clear, with no hint of the possibility of clouds moving in. It was going to be a great evening for stargazing.

I got the observatory opened up, the lights turned on, the roof opened, and everything else turned on that needed turning on. Then the students I was expecting started to show up one by one. After everybody got there, I explained what we were going to be looking at through the telescope. I let the students enter the coordinates into the telescope's controls. I watched closely and double-checked to make sure everything was done correctly. As the telescope started moving across the night sky, I checked the various monitors.

There was a folded piece of paper lying in front of one of the monitors. It had my name, "Professor Brennon," carefully printed on it. I picked it up and unfolded it. What was on the inside of the folded paper was something I had been half expecting. It was a note made up of letters cut out from various magazines.

The note read: "Your girlfriend got the first warning. This is the second warning. There may not be a third. Back off!"

The note shook me up a little because it was a direct threat against Denise as well as me. I had been threatened with bodily harm before, and while I didn't like it, the threat just increased my determination to nail the guy.

"Could I have everybody's attention please?" I called out to my students. "Thank you." They gathered around me. "There was a note lying on the work area in front of this monitor. Did anybody see it lying there when they came in, or better yet, did anybody see who laid it there?"

"I'm guilty, Professor," a student named Cristy Jones stepped forward. "Just as I was coming in, a guy stopped me and asked me to give it to you. Since I was the last one to arrive and you had already started to talk about the constellation we would be looking at, I laid the note down so I could take notes. I had every intention of giving you the note as soon as I finished taking notes, but then I kind of forgot. I'm sorry, Professor."

"That is okay, Miss Jones. Don't worry about it. You couldn't by chance describe the guy who gave you the note, could you?"

"No, I'm sorry, Professor. It was too dark. Plus, he was wearing dark clothes, and he had a baseball cap on pulled down over his eyes. The only thing I can say for sure is that he had a fairly deep voice."

"High or lower than my voice?" I asked.

"A little bit lower, I would say."

"How about height as compared to yourself?"

"He was taller than me. Around your height, I guess."

"Did you happen to notice which direction he left in?"

"It was too dark, and with his dark clothes, he just kind of melted into the darkness. I can't tell you which direction he took off in. Sorry."

"That's fine, Miss Jones. Let's all get back to doing what we came up here to do."

"I didn't do anything wrong, did I, Professor?"

"No. Not at all. I was just trying to figure out who sent me the note so I could send a reply to them. I'll figure out who sent it."

In my mind, I went over the men whom I have had the most contact with since coming to town.

Frank Duncan had a fairly deep voice, and Lord knew he was tall enough, but he had no motive for the note that I could see.

Sheriff Blocker also had a fairly deep voice, and he was tall enough. He had made it clear he didn't like civilians meddling in what he would classify as police business. I couldn't see him making threats in a note. He was too direct.

Deputy Hollister's voice would be too high.

Jack Finks didn't fit the bill because his height and voice were all wrong.

Amos Gains was a very big question mark, since I had never heard his voice. His height would be in the ballpark.

Amos and Jack both probably had the best motive. Of course, the person who composed the note could have had anybody deliver it for them.

The next day, after my morning class, I went down to the police station to hand in the note.

"Sheriff Blocker," I said, catching him as he was preparing to leave. "Can I have a minute of your time?"

"Yes, I guess," he said, leading me back to his office. "Now what can I do for you…Professor Brennon, I believe, it is?"

"Yes. Professor Brennon. I got this note last night when I was teaching a class."

I handed over the note. Blocker slipped on a pair of latex gloves before taking the note. He unfolded it and read it.

"Naturally, your prints are going to be all over this," the sheriff said with resignation.

"Sheriff," I said in exasperation, "how was I supposed to know it was going to be a threatening note? It isn't like there was a neon sign hanging above it, telling me what it was. You will also find the prints of at least one of my students on it. The name of the student is Cristy Jones."

"Calm down, Professor," the sheriff said sternly. "I guess there wasn't any way of you knowing what was in the note, but by the same token, you and Denise Cole had been warned once already. I told you then to let us handle it. But apparently, you haven't paid any attention to that warning. Now you have a second warning. The police department will do all we can to protect you, but you aren't helping matters."

"It has been how long since the first rape occurred?" I asked.

"Well, three to four months ago," he said reluctantly.

"I'm sorry, Sheriff, but taking in consideration the town's size, I feel the police should, at the very least, have somebody in custody by now. Until you do, I will keep poking around. I would much rather work with the police than get in your way. While I'm here, did you want my prints taken now for your comparison later?"

"If you have the time, now would be fine. First, I need you to tell me all the circumstances surrounding how you got the note."

I explained how the note was given to my student outside, how she brought it in, then set it down. I explained the note had lain there then until I saw it, picked it up, unfolded it, and read it. I told the sheriff what Cristy told me concerning the person who had given her the note. When he finished taking my statement, he directed me to where the booking area was. I found the area easily enough and gave the officer my prints. After I was done with that, I went back to the sheriff's office to sign my statement. "When will you see the student that gave you the note again?" Sheriff Blocker asked.

"Tomorrow."

"Would you ask her to stop here at the station at her earliest convenience? I need her prints to eliminate hers from any others there might be on the note."

"I'll talk to her and explain the situation to her."

"Thank you, Professor. You take care, and I'll get the state lab in Lincoln working on this."

I left the police station and went home to rest a little and grab a bite to eat. As I sat eating a sandwich, I got to thinking about the paper the note was pasted on. I was familiar with all grades of paper on the market. I had worked part-time in a printing company for a year while in my last year of college. At home, I kept a ream of watermarked cotton fiber laid paper to use when I really wanted to impress someone and a ream of lesser-quality paper for run-of-the mill correspondence. Unconsciously, I had taken note of the paper but hadn't given it any thought until now. As I pictured it in my mind's eye, it was brought into focus.

The base paper that the words had been pasted on was of a very good quality. I remembered it had watermark lines running up and down on the paper, about an inch apart. There were also less prominent watermark lines running across the paper that was a whole lot closer together. It was the type of bonded paper that could only be bought in a stationary store. There was only one store in Cedar Falls that would handle that grade of paper.

I looked at my watch. I figured I should have plenty of time to run down to the store before they closed. I left the house and drove down to the store. There were no other customers in the store when I walked in.

Just as I started looking through the paper section, a clerk came up and asked if she could help me find what I needed. I told her basically what I was looking for. She took me to the area that contained their bonded paper. I compared the three samples she handed me. One sample was watermarked the same way I remembered as on the note.

"Do you sell quite a bit of this paper?" I asked, indicating the one paper out of the three.

"Not a whole lot, enough that we keep it in stock. The cost keeps a lot of average people from buying it. Most of this paper is sold to business owners, but there are a few individuals that keep themselves stocked up with it."

"I don't suppose you could pull it up on your computer who them individuals would be, could you?"

"Who are you, mister?" she asked, suddenly suspicious. "If you're a cop, please identify yourself."

"No, I'm not a cop, just someone who is trying to do their bit in stopping the mayhem in Cedar Falls."

"Well, good luck, mister, but I can't risk losing my job just to satisfy your curiosity. Is there anything else I can help you with?"

"No. You have been very patient with me the way it is. Thank you." I pause a I started to turn away from her. "On second thought, I will take a ream of this paper here."

I paid for the paper and went home. I called Denise's house. She answered the phone. "Are you going to be busy this evening?" I asked.

"No. I don't have any plans. What's up?"

"I got a note last night I'll tell you about when I see you, and I'm going to need you to fire up your computer."

"I can do that. What time did you want to come by?"

"You tell me."

"Come over now, and you can have supper with Mom and me. It will just be leftovers or maybe sandwiches."

"I'm not hard to please. I'll be over in just a little bit."

I grabbed a sheet of the paper that I had just bought, locked up the house, and jumped into my Caddy. Denise was sitting on the porch when I arrived. I walked up to the porch and settled myself in the swing next to Denise.

"What is this about a note, John?" she asked, concern coloring her voice.

"Nothing to get worried about. Last night, somebody had given one of my students a note that they were to pass onto me. The student brought the note into the observatory, laid the note down instead of giving it to me right away, and then promptly forgot about it. I finally happened to see it lying there, so I unfolded it and read it. It was a second warning for me to back off on looking into the rapes and murder."

"Since this is the second threat, what are you going to do?" she asked seriously.

"I've been threatened before, Denise, but I want you to know that I do take this seriously. So far, I've been able to handle whatever anybody has thrown at me. At any rate, I took the note down to Sheriff Blocker. He wasn't very sympathetic with me after he read the note. He and I ended up having some rather heated words. He finally said he would send the note to the state lab in Lincoln for analyzing. What interested me was the paper the note was pasted on. I worked in a printing shop at one time, so I learned about different kinds and types of paper. The paper used for the note was a bonded laid paper."

"That would be a very distinguishable paper, right?" she asked.

"Yes, it is."

That doesn't make much sense to me, John. Most people who do something like that wouldn't want to call attention to the paper they used."

"Normally, I would certainly agree with you, Denise. But what if it was the only paper they had available, or they had used that paper so long that they just didn't think about the uniqueness of the paper itself. Or it could have been used as a red herring. I think it needs to be followed up on. I stopped at Knicker this afternoon. They carry the same paper. I'm very certain it's the same paper that was used in the note. Naturally, they wouldn't tell me which one of their customers buys that paper. I brought a sample along with me. How do you feel about doing a little computer hacking this evening?"

"What makes you think I know enough about computers to be able to hack into somebody else's computer?"

"I don't know if you can or not, but I'm willing to bet you have the brains to do it if you wanted to. Look at it this way. If we can find out who has access to this paper, we will probably be a whole lot closer to nailing the rapist and killer."

"Okay, I'll give it a try."

Martha came out to get us for supper then. There was fresh bread, lunch meats, cheese, ham, and all the condiments spread out on the table. After a couple of ham sandwiches and a cup of coffee, I was ready to hit the computer.

Denise and I sat down in front of the computer. I had no idea how she did it, but soon enough, she had the screen filled with the names of Knicker's customers, what they bought, and when. I asked Denise if she could narrow it down to the sales of the bonded paper. A few clicks, and she had the three bonded papers pulled up on the screen. Denise eliminated the two types of paper that I wasn't interested in. I now had a list of the users of this particular paper. I ran my eyes down the list of customers.

"This is a regular smorgasbord of who's who in town," I said appreciatively. "Let's see whom we have. There are a couple of doctors. The amount they charge, they can afford expensive paper. Several lawyers. Florence Duncan and several prominent business people are on the list. What do you think, Denise?"

"Well," she said with a shrug, "this would seem to eliminate Jack or Amos as the note writer, unless they had stolen the paper and pasted the note on the good paper with the thought in mind of throwing suspicion for the deed elsewhere. Do you think either one would be smart enough to think of that angle?"

"I would say Jack had at least an average IQ. That is my impression from talking to him. Amos, naturally, I don't have the least idea what his IQ would be. Can you print this out so we would have the information handy should we want to refer back to it at a later date? Where would Jack or Amos get any of this paper in the first place?"

"Yeah, I'll print this out. As far as Jack or Amos getting their hands on some of this paper, I might have an answer for you. Did you read in the paper that Knicker was broken into? It happened two days ago."

"The day before I got the note," I said thoughtfully.

"Yeah. I guess so. At any rate, the paper said the store was broken into after closing time. Here is the article," she said, handing me the clipping from out of her files.

"Why did you keep this article? Any special reason?" I asked as I skimmed through the article.

"No special reason. I have a habit of collecting clippings about the more interesting crimes in town. And in the past, information from these clippings has allowed me to put a bug in Ben's ear on a couple of occasions."

"This article says some merchandise was taken that amounted to several thousand dollars' worth in value. It says the safe was tampered with but that they didn't get into it. Unfortunately, the article doesn't list the merchandise taken."

"You're thinking the paper used in your note might have been from the merchandise stolen, aren't you, John?"

"You have to admit it's a possibility."

I watched as the data was downloaded out of the store's records and onto paper at our end. When it was all printed, Denise took it and filed it in her files.

"You didn't know you were that good of a hacker, did you, Denise?" I joked.

"No, and I don't plan on making a habit of doing it either."

"I wouldn't want you to either, but this is one time we might be glad we did. Well, I think I had better head for home. Thanks a lot for looking that up."

"Sure, John. You take care now, and I'll see you when we both have time."

I went home and read a book for a while to relax before turning in for the night.

The next morning dawned clear and warm. I decided to go up to the observatory and download some pictures off the computer that the students and I had taken the night we had worked in the observatory. After getting the pictures I wanted, I went up to the mansion to give the pictures to Florence Duncan as promised.

I got up to the mansion and rang the doorbell. Soon a butler appeared at the door. "May I help you, sir?" he asked stiffly.

"I would like to see Miss Florence Duncan, please. My name is John Brennon."

"If you will please wait in the library, I will see if Miss Duncan is available," the butler said, ushering me into the library and discreetly closing the double sliding doors behind me. My eyes roamed over the book-filled shelves and a couple of beautiful oil paintings.

Just then, the library doors slid open a little ways, and Frank Duncan slipped into the room, quietly closing the doors. He turned around then, and his eyes fell on me. A look of surprise flashed across his face.

"I'm sorry if I startled you, Mr. Duncan. I'm here to see your sister, and the butler put me in here to wait."

"That's okay, Professor Brennon. You really didn't startle me as much as surprised me. I wasn't expecting to finding anybody in the house but my sister, the butler, the cook, a couple of maids, and of course, myself."

"I apologize for surprising you then. I was admiring your paintings when you came in. Is the artist a local artist or someone of national or world prominence?"

"I am proud to say these paintings you see are examples of my sister's talent."

"I'm very impressed. Does she sell any of her work?"

"Not that I'm aware of. You would have to ask her."

"I'm not asking out of idle curiosity. My uncle, whose house I inherited, had a lot different tastes than I do. I have been thinking of replacing the paintings he had hung in the house with paintings more to my taste. I like what I see here."

Just then Florence came into the library through the sliding double doors.

"Ah! And here is the lady herself," Frank said with fake gallantry. "Just the artist we have been talking about."

"Professor Brennon, to what do I owe the pleasure of your visit?" she asked, ignoring her brother.

"Do you remember when you encountered me at the observatory prior to classes starting?" I asked.

"Yes."

"You said at the time you would like some interesting photos of space. The other night, I was able to get some spectacular shots that I am certain you would like to see. At least I hope you will like them."

I handed her the copies I had downloaded off the computer. She looked through them, it seemed to me, with eager interest.

"Thank you, Professor," she said warmly. "These are great, and I appreciate you going to the trouble of downloading these for me."

"I was admiring your taste in art when your brother came in. He told me you are the artist of these paintings."

"Yes, that is correct, and thank you for your admiration of my work."

"I have been wanting to change the paintings hanging in my deceased uncle's house with something else. I would like to replace them with some of your work."

"Thank you, Professor. I'm flattered that you are that fond of my work. However, it's just a hobby that I dabble in when I have time. I just paint for my own pleasure. Sorry."

"I had to try. I will be going now. You both have a good afternoon."

"And you too," they replied.

I left the mansion, grabbed a quick lunch, and then went to my classroom to get ready for my afternoon class. Soon it was time for the class to convene. I was very happy to see Cristy walk into class and was hopeful I wouldn't have too much trouble talking her into going down to the police station. Then the class was over, and the students were exiting the classroom.

"Miss Jones, could I have a word with you, please?" I called out to her. She sat down and waited for the last student to leave.

"What can I do for you, Professor?"

"It has to do with that note that was handed to you the other night. It was a threatening note to me, which I took to the police. They are sending it to a lab in Lincoln. The lab will be checking for fingerprints on the note. Since I told the police you and I had both handled the note, they need our fingerprints so they can tell which prints they need to check. I gave them my prints when I gave them the note. They asked me if I could ask you to stop at the station and leave your prints."

"I don't know, Professor," she said, shaking her head. "If I had known I was going to get into trouble, I never would have brought that note in to you."

"You aren't in any trouble, Miss Jones. None whatsoever. Your fingerprints will not go into any police file or anything like that. They will compare our prints against any lifted from the note. When they are done, they will destroy ours."

"Are you sure about that? I don't want my fingerprints stuck in any police file."

"I promise they will not get in any file, and they will be destroyed."

"When did they want me down at the station?"

"They would like you to come down as soon as you conveniently could."

"Okay, Professor. I'll go down this afternoon."

A few days later, I called Sheriff Blocker.

"Sheriff. This is John Brennon. Have you gotten anything back on that note yet?"

"As a matter of fact, the report came in just a little while ago. I am going over it now."

"So did the note writer leave any prints? Or had he watched too much TV and wore gloves to keep his prints off the paper?"

"Naturally, the note was covered mostly with yours and a couple of Miss Jones's on the outside where she handled the note while it was closed. The lab was lucky to find one print at the bottom of the page that didn't match yours or Miss Jones's. I haven't had time to put a name with the print yet, but we will be working on it."

"May I ask what files you are going to run the prints through, Sheriff?"

"The state database of known criminals first. If there are no hits there, then I'll run it through a national database."

"I don't know how close you examined the note before you sent it in to the lab, Sheriff, but I might mention that the base paper the words were pasted on is a very expensive and exclusive paper. Not many people in town use that paper because of the two factors. I have a list of the people in town who uses that note's base paper on a regular basis. Would you like for me to drop a copy of that list off to you?"

"How did you get your hands on such a list?" the sheriff asked suspiciously.

"It doesn't matter how I got it. I got it. The question is, Do you think you could make use of it?"

"I think I might have misjudged your abilities, Professor. Yes, I think it could be useful in our investigation."

"I'll drop it off this afternoon sometime. Thank you for sharing with me what the report said, Sheriff."

"Forget it. See you later with that list, or if I'm not here, just leave it with the officer at the counter."

I put the phone down and smiled. Sheriff Blocker was going to bend a little, but he wasn't about to bow all the way. But that was fine too. As long as he would allow me to work with him, maybe this case could be brought to a close faster and the criminal put behind bars a little sooner, which was what we all wanted.

I called Denise at her office and was lucky enough to catch her in. I told her I needed a copy of the paper's customer list to give to the sheriff. She asked if I told the sheriff how we got the list. I told her not to worry, that I didn't tell him how we got it nor was I going to. Denise said for me to go to her house, tell her mother what I came for, and make a copy of the list on her copying machine for the sheriff. I said I would and that I would see her as soon as I had a chance.

I went to Denise's house, and Martha answered the door. "John, it's good to see you," she said warmly. "Denise isn't home yet from the college."

"I know, Martha. I just talked to her on the phone. She said to tell you I was supposed to get a copy of a list out of her files to give to the sheriff. Okay?"

"I guess so. Are you and Denise, or the police, any closer to identifying this crook you are all chasing?"

I laid the list down on the copier I had gotten out of the files. I turned to Martha and gently gripped both of her arms up by her shoulders in my hands. I looked her straight in her eyes.

"Yes, I feel we are getting closer. And yes, it could be getting a little more dangerous. This is why I'm trying to keep Denise as far in the background and from any real danger as I can. I promise I will do everything possible in my power to protect her and keep her safe. I think a whole lot of her, Martha, and certainly don't want her to come to any harm."

"Okay, John," she said in a less worried voice. "I trust you. She is the only thing I have. I don't know what I would do without her."

"I won't let anything happen to our girl, Martha. They will have to come through me to get to her, and I'm not exactly a pushover. I have to get this list down to the police now. I'll see you later, Martha."

I took the folded list down to the police station. Sheriff Blocker wasn't in, so I left it with the officer behind the counter as instructed. The officer assured me the sheriff would get it.

That evening, there was a nice, cool autumn breeze. I called Denise and asked if she would like to go for a ride out in the country. She said she would love to. I had the top down on the car, and the air felt good as it ran its fingers through my hair as I drove over to pick up Denise.

She looked great in a sleeveless summer dress with a light sweater thrown over her shoulders. She got in, and I asked her if there was anyplace special she would like to go to. She thought for a few seconds before answering.

"There is one area that I like to go to. It's about a ten- or fifteen-minute drive from here. It's a place on the Lope Creek that is shallow enough for the water to gurgle as it flows over the rocks in the creek bed. I find the sound very relaxing."

"Lead me to it. It sounds like a place I would really enjoy too. Did I tell you that the sheriff got the report back from the lab on the note?"

"No. What did the report have to say?"

"Well, he said other than my student's and mine, the lab found one other print on the paper. He said he was going to run the print through the state database and if he didn't get any hits there, he was going to run it through the national, or federal, database."

"Hopefully, the sheriff will be able to get a hit on the print. Turn off the highway up here to your right. Yeah, right here."

I turned off the highway onto a gravel road.

"Go about a half mile. There is a rough path leading off the road on the right side. Slow down a little, John. Wait! There it is! Now turn onto this path, and it will take us to the creek. During the day, the path is very easy to see. It's a good thing there is a full moon tonight."

I turned off the road and onto the path. It was pretty much overgrown, but there had been just enough traffic on it to keep the path open. I had to go slow because of the roughness of the path. Maybe thirty or forty yards down the path, and I could hear the gurgle of the creek Denise had talked about. In the car's headlights, I easily saw the creek bank. I stopped the car, turned the engine off, and doused the lights. As Denise and I got out of the car, I grabbed my flashlight and quickly checked to see if I would be able to back around and then drive out when we left. To my relief, there was a grassy area I would be able to turn around in. Denise and I walked to the front of the car and stood side by side, listening to the music of the creek.

The car pulled up and stopped at the edge of the clearing. He was the first one there. He got out of his car and slipped the headpiece on that covered his entire head. He gathered a little bit of wood that the coven would need tonight. He stacked it up so a nice fire would be created when a match was put to it. Then the other coven members showed up while he was sitting up a folding table by where the fire would be.

The six members of the coven formed a circle around the table and the pile of wood. Also in the circle was a ten-year-old girl. Her face wasn't covered like everybody else's was.

She was covered in a cape that wrapped all the way around her body. It flowed all the way to the ground.

The high priest bent down and touched a lighter to the stack of wood. As the fire gained momentum, the high priest led the coven in prayers to Satan.

After a little bit, the ten-year-old girl was ushered up to the high priest by one of the two women occult members. The high priest picked the girl up and laid her on the table. The high priest slowly opened the cape that the girl was wrapped in to reveal the girl's naked body.

She lay there with a vacant look in her eyes. Her eyes didn't waver or flicker even when the high priest approached the table, holding a dagger with a long, slender, and sharp blade that glittered in the firelight. The coven chanted as the high priest raised the dagger over his head with the point of the blade aimed right at the young girl's chest.

"Is that wood burning I smell?" Denise asked suddenly. I sniffed the air.

"Now that you mention it, yes, I can smell wood burning too. Maybe we had better try to find out where the fire is. If it's a wildfire, we'll have to call the fire department so they can stop it from getting out of control. I have my cell phone with me."

I switched on my flashlight that I still held in my hand as Denise and I stepped away from the car. The knee-high grass that bordered the lane rustled as we advanced toward a thick stand of trees from which the smell seemed to be coming from. The ground was rough enough that I kept the beam of my flashlight close in front of us on the ground. The smell became stronger when we reached the edge of the trees.

"Is that a flicker of flames I see up ahead?" Denise asked.

"I don't know what else it would be. You can't smell smoke without something burning."

Very carefully, we advanced toward the flicker, stepping over dead limbs that had fallen out of the trees. Suddenly, I stopped dead in my tracks, firmly put my hand on Denise's arm to stop her, and put a finger to my lips.

"What's wrong, John?" she whispered.

"Listen," I commanded. We stood rock still.

"Voices," she said.

"Yeah. That's what I thought I heard too. It could be campers, but this doesn't sound like campsite sounds to me. We had better approach very cautiously."

A little further, and the flicker and voices became more distinct. A couple of yards more, and we came upon a clear area that held a scene that turned my blood to ice in my veins.

A fire illuminated four men dressed in black pants, black hoods, and black cloaks fastened at the throat with a large fastener that had the same design on it as on the button I had found at the attempted-rape scene. There were also two women dressed in the same fashion except they also wore black halter tops, whereas the men had their chests bare.

There was one more man in the group whose attire was like the other men's but with one significant difference. On his head, he wore a mask that could have been Satan's face itself.

They were chanting something in unison in low voices. Suddenly, the chanting stopped. The man in the Satan's mask announced they would proceed with the sacrifice. He lifted a dagger high in the air. The other six people bowed. A folding table was revealed with what appeared to be the naked body of an unconscious girl about ten years of age. She was to be the sacrifice.

Denise stuffed her fist in her mouth to stop a scream from exploding from her mouth. As it was, part of her scream still escaped through her clutched fist. All sounds ceased in the clearing with the exception of the crackling of the wood in the fire. The, I assumed, high priest slowly lowered the dagger. A twig snapped as Denise and I started to back away from the clearing.

"Stop!" the high priest's muffled voice commanded.

I shifted my grasp on Denise's hand to a firmer grip. I rose up, pulled Denise with me, and broke into as fast a run as the terrain permitted back through the trees and toward where the car was parked. As we ran through the trees, trying not to trip, the crashing sounds of pursuit was close behind us. Denise stumbled, but I had her hand tight enough in mine to keep her from going down.

"We're just about there, Denise. Hang in there," I urged as we broke out of the stand of trees.

The full moon lit up my white Cadillac beautifully. Denise and I sprinted toward the car through the grass. We reached the car, and Denise threw herself into the car while I slid in right behind her. I started the engine, threw it in reverse, and spun back into the grass. The bodies of all seven people swiftly approaching my car were caught in the Cadillac's headlights. I gunned the engine and twisted the wheel hard to the left. The car shot out into the lane, just missing a couple of our pursuers. We bounced down the lane, quickly leaving everybody behind in the dust.

Rage filled the mind of the high priest as he watched the car pull out of the grassy area and drive down the bumpy lane. *I know who you are, Professor John Brennon, and you, too, Miss Denise Cole*, he thought to himself. He vowed vengeance on the intruders as the car sped down the lane. Once the car was out of sight, the coven members returned to the clearing.

The girl still lay on the table like nothing had happened. "We will have the sacrifice at a later time. I will contact you and tell you where and when it will be. The two meddlesome creatures that just fled will bring other people out here tonight. We will leave now so we may worship another day."

After the high priest made his announcement, the coven members headed for their cars. The two women members took the ten-year-old girl with them. The high priest took the table down and loaded it into his vehicle. He then went back and put the fire out with the exception of a few glowing ambers. He then left, and the country night was still again.

"Are you okay?" I asked Denise once we were out of the lane and back on the gravel road.

"Yeah. I think so. I'll never get the image of that helpless girl lying there out of my mind," she said, shaking her head. "They were going to kill that poor girl in cold blood. What if they go back to that clearing and still kill her?"

"We'll go straight to the police and report what we just saw. Maybe since this coven, and it has to be the same coven Finks belongs to, was interrupted tonight, they will postpone their sacrifice at least for a little while. Maybe the police will get out here fast enough to grab one or two before they all have time to split."

We made record speed getting into town and to the police station. I parked, and we jumped out of the car and rushed into the station.

"We need help fast!" Denise said in a rush to the officer behind the counter. "A girl is about to be killed. Hurry, and you might still be able to stop it."

"Calm down, lady. You're not making sense. What girl? Who is about to kill whom?"

"A young girl about ten years old is about to be stabbed. If you guys would hurry out there, you might be able to prevent it."

"And who is about to commit this murder?"

"We don't know who they all are," I said, taking over from Denise, trying to tell the officer in a calmer voice the bare facts. "It was a group of seven people, and they are, or was, just ten minutes or so outside of town."

"A group of seven people was going to stab a girl. Have you two been drinking tonight?"

"Ben! Ben!" Denise suddenly called out.

"Denise," Ben said, coming over to the counter. "What's up?"

"We have been trying to convince your fellow officer here that a young girl is about to be murdered. He thinks John and I are drunk. Will you listen to me, Ben?"

"Sure. I'll take it, Jim."

The other officer shrugged his shoulders and walked away, saying, "They are all yours. I still think they are nuts or drunk."

"Okay, Denise. You said a young girl is about to be murdered. Where?"

"About a ten-minute drive outside of town. There is a parking spot by Lope Creek where people like to park to enjoy the sound of the creek. Off to one side of the parking spot is a stand of trees. In the middle of that stand of trees was where John and I saw them about to stab a girl, but I couldn't help but scream a little even though I tried not to. They stopped when they realized someone was watching them. We beat it out of there with them hot on our tails. We barely escaped and then came straight here."

"Okay, Denise. I want you to stay here. Would you be able to take me to the clearing where you two saw this happen, John?"

"Sure," I said readily.

"I know the spot by Lope Creek you are talking about. I've gone out there to relax myself. I just need your directions from that point to the clearing in the stand of trees."

"I'm ready to go back anytime now that at least one of us is armed."

"Okay, let's go. Sheila, will you take care of Miss Cole until we get back?" he asked a colleague.

Ben and I went out to a patrol car and got in. He drove to the parking spot by the creek. "Okay, you said this took place in the stand of trees over there?" Ben asked.

"Yeah. There is a good chance the grass will still be trampled down, so we shouldn't have much trouble following the trail to the clearing." I hesitated a couple of seconds before going on, "I know what I'm about to ask is completely contrary to police training, but under the present circumstances, it might not be a bad idea if we were both armed."

"I can't do that, John."

"Well, look at it this way, Ben, since I'll be going first, I would be right in your crosshairs in case I did anything you felt I shouldn't do. But if these people are still here, which I sincerely doubt, but if they are, you could need all the firepower you would have available."

Ben wrestled with my request for several long seconds. Finally, he made up his mind.

"Okay, but it's understood you don't pull the trigger *unless* I tell you to or to save your life or mine."

"Understood," I said. I reached in the patrol car and took the shotgun out of its holder.

I took the lead into the tall grass. The crushed and trampled grass made a perfect trail to follow. Once in the trees, the trail became a little harder to follow. A freshly scuffed bit of dirt here and there told me I was still on the track, though. Then I was at the edge of the clearing. I stopped and Ben came up to stand beside me.

The first thing to catch our attention was the glowing embers of the dying fire. We slowly moved the beams of our flashlights over the now-deserted area.

"Now you say there was a folding table set up here in the clearing with the girl they were about to kill lying on it?"

"Right, Ben, just like I told you on the way out to here. It was right here by the fire. Shall I get some more wood for the fire so we can see better?"

"I think our flashlights will be enough. There was a table sitting here not too long ago," Ben said as he ran his fingers over the ground made soft by a recent rain.

I knelt down beside Ben. My flashlight beam picked up small round shallow impressions in the grass. By running my hand over the area, I could feel where the table legs had sank about a half inch into the soft earth. The rest of the grass in the clearing was all pretty much trampled down.

"It looks to me like the people didn't follow through with the murder at least," Ben said.

"I agree. I don't see any fresh blood in the grass either."

"I don't suppose you noticed any vehicles parked that these people came out in, did you?" Ben asked as he searched the clearing in an ever-widening search pattern.

"Now that you mention it, no. I was so surprised and shocked at what I was seeing, I never gave it a thought. There must be a way in from the other direction. Otherwise, Denise and I would have walked right past their cars."

"I would say this is where they were parked," Ben said.

I walked over to where Ben was standing at the edge of the clearing opposite of where we had entered. Our flashlight beams revealed a break in the stand of trees. Double tracks in the grass clearly showed where a vehicle had been driven up and parked. We walked down the narrow lane that cut through the trees. There was evidence that several cars had been parked outside the stand of trees. Finally, after looking the area over carefully and finding nothing else, Ben and I returned to the clearing.

"I don't think we'll find anymore tonight. I'll take that shotgun now. You won't be needing it anymore tonight," Ben said, and I handed the shotgun over. "We'll go back to the station, and you and Denise can give me your statements."

We were both silent on the way back to the station. When we got there, Ben took me into an interrogation room to put my statement on a cassette tape recorder. He had another officer take Denise into another room to get her statement. After we gave our statements, Ben brought Denise into our interrogation room to wait with him and me while the statements were transcribed for us to sign.

"You two had quite a night. I'm glad you're both okay, especially you, Denise. I just can't figure out why anybody would want to kill a ten-year-old girl in cold blood. It isn't like we have organized crime in Cedar Falls, which could have made it a crime of revenge."

"This was going to be a sacrifice killing, Ben," Denise said softly.

"A sacrifice? I can't see it. A sacrifice was something that was done before Christ was nailed on the cross. I can't think of any religion in the modern world that practices sacrifice."

"Oh, there is one that does, even now," she said.

"And what religion would that be?" Ben asked in a slightly sarcastic voice.

"Satan worshipers."

"What? You've got to be kidding! Satan worshipers here in Cedar Falls? What has this guy been feeding you, Denise?"

"Are you forgetting I was out there tonight as well as John? I know what I saw. I saw how they were dressed. None of the guys were wearing three-piece suits, and the two women didn't have their Sunday best on. Plus, I did some research on the web concerning that button John had found and gave to Sheriff Blocker a while back."

"You've lost me, Denise," Ben said, holding his hand up. "What button are you talking about?"

"Do you remember when that girl was attacked over by my place by the college, Ben?" I asked.

"Yes."

"I had found a button under a hedge where the girl had been taken down. I brought it in to Sheriff Blocker. He dismissed it as nothing. Denise found out off the web that the design on that button is used by a nationwide organization, similar to how the organization of the Hell's Angels is formed, for recognition between its members. The cloak fastener of each one of them people in the group tonight bore that very same design. That tells me this coven is a charter member of this larger organization."

"It's hard to believe things like that happen anyplace, but it's really hard to believe it could happen in our little corner of the world," Ben said.

"I know what you mean. It doesn't seem possible, but I feel in any given group of people there will be a set percentage of bad people in that group. I also think when the police collars the rapist that has terrorized the town for the last couple of months that the culprit will end up being a member of this coven."

"It sure would be nice to know who the members are. With your testimony, the court could probably put them all away for tonight's attempted murder."

"I doubt it, Ben. To me, it looked like the girl had been drugged. If that was the case, she wouldn't remember a thing of what happened out there in that clearing. The court would need her testimony to really cinch an attempted-murder trial."

"If we could get our hands on just one member, we could then put pressure on the member, setting up the possibility of him or her giving up the others to save their own skin."

"Unfortunately not. Denise and I know who one of the members are. I've talked to him, and he already told me he doesn't know who any of the members are because everybody always keeps their faces covered during a meeting or ritual. So nobody knows the names of their fellow coven members."

"What's this guy's name?" Ben asked.

"I would rather not say right now. I want to keep his confidence in case he wants to pass me any information at a later date. Another reason is because he is thinking of quitting the coven, and if he does, he is going to have to move fast to escape the coven. If he does anything, though, that you would be able to prosecute him on, I will be the first to turn him in."

An officer brought Denise's and my statements in then. We read them over, signed them, and handed them back to the officer who had brought them in.

"I know you are a professor of Astronomy at the college, but have you ever had any training in law enforcement?"

"No. None whatsoever in law, like for an attorney or any type of police training. I just seem to have an aptitude for recognizing a clue when I see it and a mind that can take facts, sort them, and then put them facts in the correct order to arrive at a correct conclusion. Most of my first impressions I get of people turn out to be pretty accurate. Take, for example, the impression I got of the coven member I mentioned. He has become disenchanted with the whole thing and is ready to split. I think if they had succeeded with the killing tonight, within a few days, he probably would have turned himself in because he wouldn't have been able to handle the guilt trip."

"Listen, guys, if you two want to talk shop, please do it on your own time, at least for now," Denise broke in. "I am beat after all that has happened tonight. We are free to leave, aren't we, Ben?"

"I'm sorry, Denise. I should have realized the evening would take its toll on you. Certainly, you are both free to leave."

"Thanks a lot, Ben. We both really appreciate your investigating this tonight."

"That's okay. This is what we are here for. I'll admit I had some serious reservations about what you two were trying to tell me at first, but I don't any longer. If either one of you need anything, let me know."

"Thanks again, Ben."

We went out to the car. Denise gave a tired sigh as she dropped onto the seat.

"I know," I said apologetically. "It turned out to be not quite the evening I had planned. I had planned a nice, relaxing drive."

"It wasn't your fault how things turned out, John," she said, laying her hand on my arm for a second.

"You do realize, Denise, that we are both going to have to watch our backs a little closer. I don't know how good a look the coven got of us tonight, but they probable saw enough to know who we were. Plus, there isn't any other vintage Cadillacs in town of my Cadillac's year and model that I know of."

"I've been in similar positions before, John, and I'll be careful. I promise."

I took her home then and walked her to the door, where we were met by Martha.

"Did you two have a nice drive? I was beginning to be a little worried about whether you had run into some trouble, given the time you were gone."

"It was a nice drive, Mom. We did run into some trouble. I'll tell you all about it tomorrow morning. Right now I just want to take a shower and hit the sack. I'll talk to you later, John, and thank you for a very pleasant drive."

"Good night, Denise. Talk to you later."

Martha held on to my arm as Denise wearily climbed the stairs to her bedroom. When Denise was out of hearing range, Martha turned to me.

"Now, John Brennon, tell me what happened tonight," she demanded to know.

"We went for that drive, and Denise wanted to stop out by Lope Creek for a little while. We surprised our local coven practicing one of their rituals. They didn't like being spied on and gave chase. But as you can see, we escaped and went to the police. Denise can fill in the details tomorrow. Don't worry, Martha. Everything will be fine."

"John, a person can't live with Denise and not worry about her because she has a habit of getting herself in jams."

"Well, it has been a long evening, and I'm beat myself, so I'll bid you a good night, Martha. I'll see you later."

"Good night, John."

I left Denise's house and headed home. I glanced up at the sky and was surprised to discover the evening had clouded over. Whereas a full moon had been out when Denise and I had started the evening, the sky now looked like it could open up at any moment. About ten minutes after I got home, it started to softly rain. I grabbed a Coke out of the refrigerator and parked myself in a swing on the veranda to enjoy the soft patter of the falling rain for a while before going to bed. After turning in, I fell asleep listening to the rhythmic sound of the falling rain.

CHAPTER
SEVEN

After a quick breakfast of coffee and toast, I headed out of the house for the college. I stopped short as I walked past a patch of ground that I had engaged the local nursery to rototill and seed with grass seed. Even though it had been several days since the work had been done, the ground was still soft enough that when someone had stepped on it, they left their footprint. The footprints led right up to the veranda. Small bits of dirt on the veranda led to a living room window.

I carefully checked the window and window casing for signs of attempted forced entry. I found some scratches in the wood of the window in the area of where the window's lock was. The window had a good fit to it, which prevented the prowler from getting to the lock without breaking the glass. I credited the small notice in the window, which read "Caution: Premises protected by ADT," for saving the window from being broken.

However, if I was lucky, the prowler might have left a fingerprint or two. I would have to give Ben a call and see if he could dust the window for prints.

I then went back to the footprints in the dirt. I grabbed a ruler I carried in my briefcase and measured the length and width of the print. It measured thirteen inches long. From the depth of the print, the condition of the soil and the wetness of the soil, I estimated the prowler to be around 6 feet to 6 feet and 4 inches tall and 190 to 220 pounds.

The sole part of the shoe the intruder was wearing was smooth, like something that would be found on an oxford or dress shoe. The heel print showed nothing special. I had seen the same design on shoes in the shoe store. They were expensive shoes to be sure, but still shoes available to the general public.

Since there was nothing else to be learned from the footprints, I locked up the house, backed the car out of the garage, and proceeded to my classroom at the collage. After calling the police station and finding out Ben wouldn't be on duty until that afternoon, I made preparations for my class later in the morning. By the time the class was over, it was close to lunchtime. I was stepping out into the hall to stretch my legs when Martin Land, professor of meteorology, whose classroom was next to mine, also stepped out into the hall.

"Good morning, John," he said, warmly coming over to me. "Haven't seen much of you lately."

"Just been busy, Martin. There are a lot of things to do getting a new department set up and running."

"It couldn't be that somebody else is taking up quite a bit of your time, could it?"

"I'm sorry, Martin, but I don't have the least idea whom you could mean. I haven't been here long enough to fill my little black book yet. I'm not seeing anybody at the present."

"The rumor mill has it that Denise Cole and you spend quite a bit of time together."

"She was the first friend I made in this town. Sure, I like her a lot but only as a good friend. There is nothing more between us."

"Okay. I hear you. How about your crime-fighting endeavors? Are they bearing any fruit?"

"I have a short list of people I suspect to be the rapist and killer, just no positive proof yet. I have to run right now, Martin. See you around."

"Sure, John. Take care, and I'll see you around."

I thought about how my friendship with Martin had developed since I met him. We met the second day after classes started, and I had gone to his classroom to borrow a magic marker. Over time, I found that a lot of his views coincided with my own views. He was also single like me.

I decided to go down to the police station instead of calling again. When I got there, I asked for Deputy Hollister at the front counter. The officer said Ben wasn't in yet. I saw Detective Jerkins then and called him over. I told him who I was, and he informed me he already knew who I was.

"Last night, Detective, I had a prowler at my house. I didn't know until this morning when I saw their footprints. They tried to jimmy a window but didn't succeed in getting in. However, I'm hoping maybe they left some fingerprints behind. Do you think it would be possible for you to come over and dust for prints?"

"I'll have to clear it with the sheriff, but I should be able to do it this afternoon. Which window did the prowler try to jimmy?"

"The living room window to the left of the front door. You will see the scratches in the wood of the window. And thank you, Detective."

A couple of days later, I was downtown and stopped at the police station. "Is Detective Jerkins in?" I asked the officer behind the counter.

"Yes. Hold on, and I'll see if he can see you now."

He went over to an unmarked door and stuck his head in. He had his head in for a few moments, pulled it out, and motioned for me to come over. I did, and the officer ushered me into Detective Jerkins's office.

"I'm guessing you are here to ask if I found any prints on your window."

"You are absolutely correct, Detective."

"Yes, as a matter of fact, I was able to get a full set of prints off your window. I compared them to the one print we got off that note. One print matched."

"That means the same person who sent me that note and my prowler last night was one and the same. He must be getting scared, careless, or just doesn't care that much anymore to leave a full set of prints behind. You never did get a hit when you ran that one print through the state and federal databases, did you?"

"No, I'm afraid that was a wash. But even though we didn't get any hits, we now have a full set of prints to work with. You never know, someone could be arrested at any time and turns out to be the owner of these prints."

"Okay, Detective Jerkins. Thank you very much."

I left the police station and went home to work on my lesson plan for the next week. It was early evening when I got the lesson plans done. I decided to take a walk in the park. The park was only four blocks from my house. George McAllister was working in his front yard as I started to walk by.

"Good evening, Mr. Brennon," he called out. "How are you doing?"

"Good evening, George. Just call me John. I'm doing pretty well. Keeping busy."

"Did you ever hear what happened with that girl that was attacked here in my yard?"

"Her injuries luckily wasn't that serious. I visited her in the hospital after it happened. I heard she moved out of town shortly after she was released from the hospital. I really don't blame her if she did."

"I wouldn't either. So out for a little walk this evening?"

"It's such a nice evening it just seemed like the thing to do."

"That it is. Have a good walk, John."

An hour before I left the house, another well-dressed man carrying an overnight bag leisurely entered the park. The park was empty at the moment, but there was a girl that liked to stroll through the park just after dusk pretty often. He had been watching her, fantasizing about what he would do when he got her in his power. It was a beautiful evening, the kind of evening she liked to walk in.

He went over behind some bushes that would serve as cover for him but still allowed him to keep an eye on who came into the park. He smoked a couple of cigarettes in anticipation of what he was hoping would happen. He then changed into an all- black outfit that covered him from head to toe, helping him hide in the night. He set aside the overnight bag, which had carried his all-black outfit and now had his other clothes, making sure it was somewhere he could grab it fast.

Here she is, he thought excitedly as he watched the very pretty blond-haired girl start to make her trip through the park. Just as she got even with an extra-large clump of bushes, he sprang. In one swift practiced move, he had the girl pulled to the ground and dragged into the bushes. One hard blow to her chin, and she was unconscious.

Savagely he lifted her skirt up to around her slim waist and tore her panties off her body. He tore her blouse open to drink in the sight of her bra-covered breasts with crazed, cruel eyes.

After he satisfied his lust, he produced a slender, sharp dagger. He touched the point of the dagger to the girl's throat then drew it to one ear. The fire of hell burned in his eyes as he drew the dagger across the girl's neck. The sight of the blood flowing from the cut was like food to a starving person.

He was jolted out of his state of bliss by the sound of a cough not too far from where he was. He looked up and saw a guy walking through the park. He grabbed his bag, jumped up, burst from the bushes, and ran toward some bushes in a darker part of the park. He knew he would be able to escape through them.

After making his escape, he found a dark corner in a backyard of a house that was dark and had no barking dog. He quickly changed back into his street clothes he had on before. He sauntered out of his hiding place and out to the sidewalk. He watched as the person who had flushed him earlier went into the park followed by a patrol car. He stood there waiting for the inevitable to happen. And then it did. The wail of the patrol car's siren, a shout for someone to stop, and a figure streaking out of the park.

There's no more entertainment here tonight, so I might as well go home, he decided.

I leisurely walked to the park. The sun had sunk well below the horizon. Just as I entered the park, a patrol car also entered the park on patrol. I strolled through the picnic area, heading toward a clump of bushes about six feet high, while the patrol car drove through the park, coming up behind the clump of bushes.

Suddenly, a man dressed all in black burst from the bushes, running. The officer in the patrol car turned his flashing lights and siren on. The man from the bushes rushed at me like he was crazed. When he got closer, I recognized him.

It was Jack Finks! "Jack! Stop!" I cried out.

Jack acted like he never heard me. As he ran past me, I tackled him around his legs. We crashed to the ground with me on top of him. He kicked and clawed the ground, trying to get away. The patrol car stopped, and Ben jumped out and came flying over. I made the mistake of relaxing my grip around his legs a little. It was enough for Jack to kick me off him. He twisted away from Ben and me. In a flash, he was up and running again. Even though it just took Ben and me a few seconds to get back on our feet, Jack was nowhere to be seen.

"Where in the hell did he go?" Ben asked.

"I have no idea. Once he got loose, he was gone in a flash. It doesn't help as dark as it's getting either. What do you think made him run like that?"

"I don't know. Let's find out."

Ben grabbed a flashlight out of his patrol car, and we proceeded over to the clump of bushes. It didn't take long to find the body lying in the bushes.

It was the body of a fully clothed girl about twenty-two years old. She was wearing a skirt and blouse. The skirt had been pushed up around her slim waist, and her panties had been ripped off. Her blouse was partly open. And then there was the matter of her throat. It had been slit from ear to ear. She had been dead long enough for the blood to have stopped flowing.

"Deputy Hollister requesting backup and an ambulance in the west end of the park," Ben said into the mic clipped to his shirt.

"Roger that," came the reply over his radio.

Within five minutes, a couple of other patrol cars and the ambulance came screaming into the park. Ben started to give the other officers what description he could of Jack. I waited until Ben was done before saying anything.

"The name of the guy you are looking for is Jack Finks."

Ben finished filling the other officers in briefly on what happened and in what direction Jack had taken off in. Sheriff Blocker had been standing in the back of the other officers, listening. When they dispersed to their respective patrol cars, the sheriff stepped forward.

"Mr. Brennon, you said the name of the guy that got away was Jack Finks. How do you know him?"

"I found a picture of him in an old high school yearbook, which is where I got his name. I tried looking his name up in the phone book, found that he still lived in town, and went to see him."

"What had you gone to see him about?"

"Remember when that other girl was attacked a couple of doors down from my house?"

"Yes. But what has that got to do with Finks, unless you think he committed that crime too?"

"The guy that tried that was too tall and big to have been Finks. But what I was going to say was that I had found a button under the bushes and brought it in to you."

"It was just a plain, ordinary button."

"Not quite, Sheriff. I was able to trace, through that button, Finks's involvement in a coven of Satan worshippers that operate right here in Cedar Falls. At any rate, I talked to Finks because I'm convinced the person behind all this is a member of this coven. Finks might be the one who committed the first rapes and murders, and he looks guilty as sin on this one, but he wasn't the guy I had chased away, the one who had attacked that girl over by my house."

"I read your statement about what you and Miss Cole said you saw outside of town the other night. I still don't know if I agree with your conclusions on the proposed killing being a sacrifice."

"That is your privilege, Sheriff. Eventually, you will find it out to be fact—a fact that the sooner you accept, the faster you will probably solve who is behind what has been happening in town."

"Sheriff, can we take the body now?" one of the men off the ambulance asked.

"No. Wait a second. I want to look it over before it's moved."

I followed the sheriff over to the girl's dead body. He started by examining her head. There were a few scratches on her face. I figured she got these from the bushes while struggling with her assailant. Her throat appeared to have been cut in one smooth motion. There were scratches on her arms, which I attributed also to the bushes. There were bruises on each arm where she had been held down or where she was initially grabbed.

Her blouse had been ripped open. With her raised skirt and removed panties, rape was a foregone conclusion. There were also bruises around her vagina and on her thighs.

Something was bothering me about the girl's blouse. I examined her blouse closer. I finally picked out what it was that had been bothering me. There was a small smudge of some kind of paint on her blouse. It would have been very easy to miss because it was just a shade different than the color of the blouse.

"Did you notice this paint on her blouse, Sheriff?" I asked, pointing to the spot.

"No. I didn't," he said, looking at it. He lightly touched the paint. "Hollister! Bring me an evidence tag. This looks and feels like an oil-based paint to me. Forensics will be able to identify it for us."

"An oil-based paint," I said softly, thinking out loud. "Do you think it could be the type of paint an artist would use?"

"It could be that kind of paint, I guess," the sheriff agreed.

Just then, Detective Jerkins arrived and came over to us. He knelt down and quickly scanned the dead girl's body.

"Damn," he said with disgust in his voice. "It had been quite long enough since that last rape attempt I had hoped the maniac had taken his business elsewhere."

"It doesn't look like we're going to be that lucky," the sheriff said. "Did you want to examine the body before I have them take her?"

"Go ahead and let the ambulance crew have her."

Sheriff Blocker put bags on her hands to preserve any evidence she might have scratched off her assailant. He also attached the evidence tag to her blouse, marking the spot of the paint. He then turned the body over to the ambulance crew. After the ambulance left, the sheriff and detective started to look the crime scene over. I also looked the scene over best I could without a flashlight, being very careful to not get in anybody's way. Finally, the police was finished with the crime scene and started to pack up to leave.

"Sheriff Blocker," I said to him before he got away, "would you mind telling me who does your autopsies in town?"

"We only have a couple of doctors in Cedar Falls, and they are general practitioners. Neither one of them have the qualifications to practice pathology medicine. So when we need an autopsy done or need any type of forensic investigation done, I send the body to Lincoln for the autopsy and request a forensic team from Lincoln when I need that."

"How long does it usually take to get a report back from them?"

"A few days to a couple of weeks, depending on the complexity of what they are looking for and what they initially find. But then you should know that police records aren't public information."

"I'm aware of that fact, Sheriff. On this, I don't see what the report would say anyhow that we can't already see for ourselves, except for DNA evidence. I was thinking more of down the road. We could probably help each other at no expense to the department."

"We'll see," Sheriff Blocker said. "I've never approved of any civilian involving themselves in police business, but you have proved to be somewhat of an exception. So we'll see."

I let the matter lie and left the park to walk home. I passed a few people on the sidewalk, mostly students from the college. When I passed a group of laughing girls, I marveled at how carefree they all appeared. Maybe none of them realized how vulnerable they really were, or maybe it was just the feeling of invincibility that younger people all seemed to have. Whatever the reason, I sincerely hoped nothing would ever happen to any of them to shatter their peaceful, ordered world.

I got home, went in, and turned the living room light on. I found myself looking into the frightened eyes of Jack Finks. He was tensely sitting on the edge of the couch seat. There were wet spots on his black shirt.

"What in the hell are you doing here, Jack?" I yelled at him.

"I'm scared, Professor, real scared."

"You should be. Is that blood on your shirt?"

"Blood?" he echoed, looking down at his shirt like it was the first time he had ever seen it. "No! I mean, yes! But I didn't kill her. You've got to believe me!"

"How did you know she was dead if you didn't kill her?"

"I couldn't see it, but I could feel the gash on her neck. I felt so much blood. She had to be dead."

"Calm down, and start at the beginning. Why were you in the park, and what were you doing there?"

"I go to the park quite often for the solitude of the place," he said after taking a deep breath. "That is why I was there. As far as what I was doing, I wasn't doing nothing, just walking and enjoying the quiet. I wasn't doing nothing."

"Go on," I prompted. "What happened next?"

"I got close to the bushes, and suddenly somebody jumps up out of them and takes off like the devil himself was on their tail."

"Can you describe this other guy or tell me what he was wearing?"

"I couldn't see him too well because of it being dark, but it seemed like he was fairly tall and he was dressed all in black, including his face."

"Why are you dressed all in black, Jack?"

"I just like black!"

"Okay. Go on."

"Well, after the guy took off, I looked into the bushes just out of curiosity. When I couldn't see anything, I went into the bushes, and that was when I felt the body of the girl. I was petrified. I just froze for what seemed like forever. Then when the cop came into the park and drove over by me, I panicked and ran. That is when, I guess it was you, tackled me."

"Why did you come here? There really isn't much I can do to help you."

"Because I had to tell somebody what happened who might believe me. I don't know if you do, but I figured you would be my best chance of anybody believing me. I swear I never killed her, but the police isn't going to believe me. You do believe me, don't you, Professor?" he begged me.

"I'll think about it. How did you know where I live?"

"After we talked that first time, I felt I might be able to turn to you if I needed help. I followed your car to the college one day, and after asking around a little, I got your name. I called information and got your address from them."

I had been so engrossed in listening to Jack that I failed to notice the bay of bloodhounds until they were right outside the house. A loud banging on the door startled Jack and I both.

"Open up, this is Sheriff Blocker. The house is surrounded."

"What am I going to do?" Jack asked, looking around wildly for an escape.

"Nothing. You are going to go with the police quietly. There isn't any escape. I will keep trying to get to the bottom of this mess, and if you are telling me the truth, you will be cleared."

"Everybody, come out with your hands up!" the sheriff demanded.

"Okay, Professor. I'll go quietly."

I went to the door and opened it. Immediately the sheriff and a deputy rushed in with guns drawn. The sheriff had Jack covered, while the deputy had me covered.

"Now both of you stand real still," the sheriff ordered. He walked over to Jack. "Put your hands behind your back." Jack complied. "You are under arrest for murder. Let's go."

"What about him?" the deputy asked, gesturing toward me.

"Take this guy on out to the patrol car. I'll talk to the professor in here."

After everybody left the room, Sheriff Blocker and I sat down in the living room.

"Okay, Professor, suppose you tell me why Finks, I believe that's his name, made a beeline for your house after murdering that girl in t he park?"

"I really don't know why he came here. It was a complete surprise to me when I got home and found him here in my living room. What he said to me was that he was scared, that he didn't kill the girl, and that the police wouldn't believe him. He claims somebody else was in the bushes with the girl before he even knew she was there. When this other guy ran, that's when Finks claims he found the girl. He then panicked when Ben entered the park in his patrol car and drove up to the bushes where the girl's body and he were. He then ran himself. He might have come here, too, because I had talked to him once before. Do you really think he committed the rape and murder tonight?"

"He has blood on his clothes. He was in the bushes with the dead body. All we need is DNA evidence off her body that matches his DNA, and we will have an airtight case. I have no doubt that we will find the DNA match linking him to the crime."

"I don't know, Sheriff. He was really shook up tonight. I believe he could commit any number of crimes, maybe even rape, but murder? I can't see him doing that."

"Well, forensics will settle the question one way or the other. In the meantime, don't plan on taking any trips. I might want to talk to you again."

"I'll be right here, Sheriff."

The sheriff left, and I locked the house up for the night. It had been a long day. I was tired, so I took a nice long shower and hit the sack.

The next couple of days, I was kept busy with class business. I called Denise on Saturday to see if she would like to have lunch with me. She said she would, so I picked her up, and we ended up at Jim's Cafe for lunch.

"I'm sorry I haven't had a chance to talk to you, Denise, for several days, but I've been pretty busy. How have things been going for you?"

"Pretty good, John. Been keeping busy myself. Have you had a chance to read the paper?"

"No."

"There was another girl raped and murdered in the park a couple of nights ago. Since they said she didn't have any identification on her, the police put a picture of her in the paper, asking if anybody recognized her. Unfortunately, I did. She was one of my best students. Her name was Doris Lamb. She had plans of becoming a symphony orchestra conductor."

"Did the article mention Jack Finks was arrested for the rape and murder?"

"Yes, it did. How did you know, John? You said you hadn't seen the paper recently."

"I was in the park when Jack made a break for it. He escaped, and then he showed up at my house, where Sheriff Blocker arrested him.

Just out of curiosity, you don't happen to know how her tuition was paid or by whom, would you?"

"Why would you ask that, John?"

"Last night, while the sheriff was looking her body over, I got a chance to look it over too. I could see that the skirt and blouse she was wearing were on the threadbare side. I figured she was just getting by. Girls are much more particular about their clothes than guys."

"It's on the ironic side that she was one of the few students that I got fairly close to. She was a hard worker, which was something I really admired about her. She told me she had received a partial scholarship. Her folks sent her some money each month, and she worked part-time."

"Where did she work part-time?"

"She was a part-time maid for Florence Duncan."

"Really!" I exclaimed. "Frank Duncan mentioned his sister had a couple of maids when I was at the mansion that time I saw him in the library. I wonder how she happened to get the job."

"The way I understand it, the people in Admissions at the college has been told to keep an eye open for scholarship students. When the Admissions Office finds somebody and Duncan has an opening, the office sends the student up to the mansion for a job interview. If the student gets the job, Duncan sets it up where the hours the student works at the mansion don't interfere with their class schedule. Doris said she liked working for Duncan."

"Did she by chance say what her hours and days were that she worked as a maid?"

"She didn't elaborate on it, but she did mention she normally worked Tuesdays after classes and the weekend, during the day."

"That means she didn't work the day she was killed. Let's go down to the park after we finish eating. It was pitch dark the night she was killed. You never know, we might find something the police missed."

"Why not? It's a nice day. Besides, I don't have anything else to do today."

We finished our lunch, left Jim's, and jumped into the car. When we got to the park, I pointed out to Denise where Doris's body had been found and the route Jack took when he ran. I parked the car, and we got out and walked over to the clump of bushes.

We started to go over the area with a fine-toothed comb. Where Doris's body had lain, there was a dark stain on the ground. It was where Doris's life had drained out of her. A few of the small branches and twigs of the bushes were snapped from when she was dragged through them. Since I didn't know what direction the first guy, according to Jack, had taken off in, Denise and I fanned out and started to search the ground leading away from the direction Jack had fled in. I had pretty much given up hope of finding anything when suddenly Denise called out.

"John! Come over here. I think I might have found something."

I hurried over to where she was standing. She pointed to a couple of crushed cigarette butts that looked to be fresh.

"Do you think if the killer had sat waiting for a victim to come his way, he might have smoked a couple of cigarettes?"

"Do you know how much the park is used after dark?" I asked.

"It used to be that a lot of people in town would walk through the park in the evening, but with all the rapes as of late, I think traffic has slowed considerably. Doris told me once how she enjoyed walking through the park because it was close enough to the college that it made for a nice walk without wearing her out. I advised her it wasn't safe to walk in the park or even on a dark street alone until the rapist operating in town was caught. She replied with those famous last words: 'I can take care of myself.'"

"Did Doris smoke?"

"No."

"I think you are right. I think these are from the killer. The weather hasn't had a chance to deteriorate them yet."

I pulled a small envelope out of my pocket. I carefully picked up the butts on the bent edge so as to leave as little of my own prints on them as possible. The name on the cigarette paper was a name I had never heard of. Denise said she could check on the web and see if it was a premium brand made in the United States. I gave the butts to Denise so she would have the name handy when she checked on the internet.

"You know, Denise, there was one thing we were going to do but never did because other things sidetracked us."

"And what was that?" she asked.

"We were going to check and see what kind of trouble Florence said her brother, Frank, had gotten into in the past. I guess the reason I'm thinking of it now is, I happen to remember he was smoking that night I surprised him outside the Duncan mansion and thought he was a prowler. He would be the kind of person to smoke an exotic brand if for no other reason than for the attention it would get him. I could check the courthouse records to see what I could find."

"What do you want me to do other than check this brand on the internet?"

"Could you check with Ben and maybe find out if the police had gotten the autopsy and forensic reports back yet on Doris?"

"Sure. I know Ben was going to be out of town this weekend, but I can call him Monday and see what he says. Why don't you come over to the house now? I'll fire up the computer, and we'll see what we can find."

"Okay. I'll even take you and your mother out for dinner after we're done on the computer. How does that sound?"

"Fine by me. When are you going to the courthouse?"

"I have all day Monday free. My class is going to be working in the observatory Monday night. I can call you around six o'clock to see if you were able to get anything from Ben."

"That will be fine, John. Right now let's go home and see what we can find on the old internet."

We left the park, and I drove over to Denise's house. Martha was happy to see me, so I spent a little time talking to her and rubbing the ears of Denise's dog, Shadow. Finally, Denise and I got settled in front of the computer. It took Denise a while to narrow the search down from general tobaccos and brands down to the brand on the butts.

"The cigarette is of a Turkish and American blend of tobaccos. They are produced right here in the United States. The price of them, though, is double the price of the highest priced regular brands you can pick up anyplace. They are available only from this one place in New York City," Denise said.

"Try to hack into their customer file," I urged Denise.

She tried but ran into a brick wall no matter what she tried. "Either they don't keep the names of their customers in the computer or they have a very sophisticated computer system or I just can't hack well enough. Whatever the reason, we won't get the names of their customers off the net. It looks like we'll just have to keep our eyes open."

The rest of the afternoon and evening I spent relaxing and enjoying Denise and her mother's company. In the course of our conversation, I discovered that Denise was an only child. Her father had died in a car accident involving a drunk driver when they lived in New York City. Denise was in her midteens when the tragedy occurred. Her father had provided for the family well enough for Martha to send Denise to college. Denise was offered the job at Duncan College several years after she graduated. She and Martha moved to Cedar Falls, and they said they had loved living here ever since.

I in turn told them I had been married before coming to Cedar Falls. The marriage had ended in a messy divorce. When I heard about Duncan College wanting to start an Astronomy Department, I applied for the job and got it. Originally, I was raised on a farm, but in my senior year of high school, my parents moved to Dallas, Texas. I attended college in Texas and worked as an assistant professor at a junior college before ending up here in Cedar Falls."

"Now that you have been here for a while, how do you like living in a smaller town as compared to a large city?" Martha asked.

"I really like living here. The people are a lot friendlier than in a big city. I plan on living here a good long time unless the astronomy thing doesn't work out at the college and they fire me. Well, I see it's getting late, so I will take my leave and say good night. Thank you both for a very pleasant afternoon and evening."

"We always enjoy it when you come around, John," Martha said. "Take care and come back soon."

Denise walked me out to the car.

"I'll give you a call toward Monday evening," I said.

"Okay, John. Take care."

I went home, took a shower, and climbed into bed.

Sunday dawned clear and with just a little nip in the air—a good day to do some winter preparation in the yard.

Monday morning, I got up a good half hour before the courthouse opened and had a good breakfast. I found plenty of parking spots in front of the courthouse. I parked and went inside to the department that had the public records. I asked for court records of traffic violations and misdemeanor violations for anybody named Duncan. When the clerk asked for a first name, I lied and said I didn't have a first name to go with the last name.

I found that over the space of several years, Frank Duncan had accumulated several speeding tickets and a couple of reckless-driving tickets. Around noon, I had exhausted that area of investigation. I next asked for the records of any felony offenses of Duncan.

After several more hours of careful examination, I was able to compile a short list offenses by Frank Duncan. He had been brought to trial for rape once, but the charges were dismissed for lack of evidence. He also had been brought to trial for terroristic activities, but again the charges were dropped due to the lack of evidence. I wrote down the date of the trial on the terroristic charge. My next stop would have to be the library to check back issues of the paper.

I sat there for a few moments, digesting this new information. This kind of publicity would really hurt a person in Florence Duncan's position in the community. I understood now why she wanted her brother to leave town as soon as possible. With this kind of personal history, whether it be yours or a relative's, dogging you, I couldn't help but wonder what it was that was keeping Frank in the area.

I gathered all the records up that I had examined and returned them to the clerk. I left the courthouse and went over to the library. I walked in and found Judy on duty.

"Hello, Judy," I said. "I don't know if you remember who I am or not."

"If I remember right, you are that professor friend of Denise's."

"Right. I need the back newspaper copies for the six-month period between these dates," I said, giving her a note with the dates written down.

"Go on over to machine 2, and I'll bring the microfilm over to you."

"Thanks, Judy."

She brought the microfilm of the latest date that I had written down first. I put the microfilm in the machine and started my search. The first couple of hours yielded nothing but what you would expect out of a paper for a town of this size.

Then I came across the story I had been looking for. The report said a girl of eighteen was found staggering on the highway just outside town. She was brought into the hospital, where she was diagnosed as suffering from a traumatic experience. When the doctors had gotten her sufficiently calmed down, she told the sheriff a wild story. She claimed she had accidentally stumbled upon some type of occult activity. The head guy made it seem like he was going to kill her. She acted like she had fainted and was able to escape. When asked if she could identify any of the people involved, she claimed the head guy was Frank Duncan. She said Duncan had dated her several times and that she had recognized Frank's voice as the voice of the top man. Frank was arrested and then released on bail. When it came to trial, the girl recanted her testimony on the witness stand, which resulted in Frank being released with all charges dropped due to lack of evidence. An article a week later, said the girl had left town.

By this time, the afternoon was pretty well shot. I gathered up all the microfilm and took them back to Judy.

"Did you find what you were looking for, Professor?" she asked.

"Yes, I think I did. Thank you."

"You're welcome."

I left the library, went home, and gave Denise a call. "How did it go at the courthouse?" she asked.

"Our boy Frank wasn't a Boy Scout. He had a few speeding and one reckless-driving violation, but then there probably isn't a driver out on the road that hasn't had a speeding ticket. What interested me were the trials for rape and terroristic activities."

"Boy, he sounds like a real nice guy."

"Doesn't he, though? The frosting on the cake, for him at any rate, was that he beat both charges due to lack of evidence. In the terroristic-activities case, the one lone witness recanted her testimony when she got on the witness stand. Then she left town shortly after the trial."

"You know what it sounds like to me?" she asked.

"I know what it sounds like to me, but I'm curious what it does sound like to you."

"It sounds to me that either Frank himself or Florence, since she is the only family he has that we know of, bribed this girl to change her testimony. I'm sure Florence has enough money to pay a good price to make a blemish like that on the family name disappear."

"From what you've told me, Frank doesn't appear to work, so I doubt if he would have much money of his own to pay a bribe. I am surprised the court records showed as much as they did on the terrorist case."

"I just got the bare facts there. I got the rest of the information from back issues of the paper at the library. And I agree with your assessment about what probably happened with the witness. Were you able to talk to Ben today?"

"Yeah. I talked to him early this afternoon. The police had gotten the two reports back just this morning. The autopsy showed the slit throat was the cause of death. She bled to death. She was definitely raped, but the rapist had used a condom because they didn't get any sperm out of her. However, they did get skin out from under her fingernails, so they were still able to get a DNA sample of her attacker. On the forensic side, they checked that paint that was on her blouse. It was oil-based paint, the kind of paint that artists use, which is sold in several stores in town."

"Well, I was right on that deduction. Oh, oh, I just looked at my watch. I better get over to the observatory so I'll be ready for tonight's class."

"Okay, John. You have a good evening stargazing, and I'll see you later when we have more time."

I hurried over to the observatory, got the top opened up, and made all the necessary preparations for the class. When my students all got there, I moved the telescope to a specific constellation. The class then had to identify the constellation and make a diagram of it. After an enjoyable evening of looking up at the heavens, it was time to dismiss the class. After getting everything turned off and the top closed, I stepped out of the observatory to lock up and leave. To my surprise, Frank Duncan was strolling around under the bright lights of the parking area, looking my car over intently.

"Good evening, Mr. Duncan. What can I do for you?" I asked, approaching him.

"Good evening, Professor. I had gone for a walk, and when I saw your car parked here, I had to stop and admire it. I think this year

Cadillac was the best-looking Cadillac General Motors made. But where did you ever find one in this good a shape?"

"I found the car in a junkyard and was able to pick it up for next to nothing, Mr. Duncan."

"Call me Frank," he insisted.

"Okay. It took a couple of years and quite a bit of money to put it back into mint condition. And you probably know should you get in an accident with this you would be as safe in this as you would be in a tank just about, barring being T-boned."

As we talked, Frank took out a pack of cigarettes and lit one up. My nose twitched as his cigarette smoke drifted my way. It had a fragrance unlike any tobacco I had ever smelled before.

"Could I ask you what brand of cigarette you are smoking, Frank?" I asked.

"Sure. It's a special brand that I doubt you had ever heard of. I send away for them."

"The name of the brand wouldn't be Holstens by chance, would it?"

"Yes. That is the name of them," he answered in a surprised voice.

"And you get them from a tobacco store in New York City?" I pressed.

"Yes, you are right as to the brand name of them and where I get them from. But how did you get the name of them and where to get them from?" he asked in a slightly menacing voice.

"It really doesn't matter, does it? Let's just say I get around. And I'll bet there isn't anybody else in town that smokes that brand. Just out of curiosity, how did you ever run across the brand?"

"I travel quite a bit and came across the brand when I was in New York City. They are a little on the expensive side, but I have a feeling you already know what they cost. But then, if a person can afford a better quality of something, why not indulge yourself a little bit? Life is too short not to, don't you agree?"

"I agree to a degree. What really is important is what a person does with their life. You can be a positive contributor to society or a menace to society. Everybody has a choice. I chose to do the positive thing myself."

"And that is grand, Professor. I really must be running along now. It's way past my bedtime. You take care, Professor, and watch your back. You never know who is back there."

I watched as he disappeared into the dark night. I pondered what Frank had just said. After everything that had happened recently, along with the facts that Denise and I had dug up, I figured Frank's advice was good advice.

The next morning, I had my regular morning class. After class, I went down to the police station and asked to see Jack Finks. The officer put me in a windowless, mirrorless room. He returned a few minutes later with Jack in handcuffs. The officer cuffed Jack to the table and stepped out of the room.

"How are things going, Jack?" I asked.

"About as good as can be expected in jail. What's happening out there?"

"If you told me the truth, and I believe you did about there being another guy, you should be cleared as soon as your DNA report comes in. They have taken a DNA sample from you, haven't they?"

"I don't know. How do they take a DNA sample?"

"They can use a swab in your mouth, get it off a bottle you had drank out of, or they can use a urine sample, a blood sample, or any other number of ways."

"They took a blood sample. They said they needed it to check for any drugs or alcohol in my system. They won't find anything because I don't do drugs and I hadn't had anything to drink that night. Is that the sample you mean?"

"Probably."

"Why would they want my DNA?"

"There was a little bit of skin under the murdered girl's fingernails. I don't think you have any scratches on you, do you?"

"I got a couple of scratches on my arms when I jumped out of the bushes, but they were made by the bushes, not the girl."

"Once they compare your DNA against what they recovered from under her fingernails, you should be cleared then. What are your plans when you are released?"

"I want to get as far away from this place as I possibly can."

"The police may not let you leave town right away. Even when the DNA clears you, you will still be considered a person of interest. I wouldn't plan on leaving town right away."

"Thanks, Professor, for keeping me up to date. It makes me feel a lot better."

"Sure, Jack. You take it easy. Do exactly what they tell you to do, and you'll be out before you know it. I have to go now."

I left the police station and went home to do some class paperwork. After I was done, I decided to go over to Denise's. She was sitting on the porch, enjoying the cool evening.

"Good evening, John. What brings you over this way?"

"No reason in particular. I had gotten some class paperwork done and decided to wander over this way. I'm not interrupting anything, am I?"

"Not a thing. Mom went over to a friend of hers, and I was just enjoying the evening. So what have you been up to?"

"Not too much. I talked to Frank Duncan last night after my class. Then I went downtown and talked to Jack Finks at the jail this afternoon."

"And what did Finks have to say?"

"The police took a blood sample from him. When they compare his DNA against what they got from under Doris's fingernails, he will either be turned loose or held for trial. I still don't think he did it."

"And what about Duncan? Did he have anything interesting to say?"

"Not too much. He had come down to the observatory to admire my car. He does smoke that brand of cigarette that we found in the park. He didn't admit to being in the park at any time, but he did tell me to watch my back."

"He threatened you?"

"Indirectly. He really doesn't worry me, though. I have been threatened before. But I will be a little more cautious now."

"How do you think the Astronomy Department is coming now that we have had several weeks of school?" she asked.

"The kids in this class seem to be very enthusiastic about it. What's the scuttlebutt that you've heard?"

"I've overheard some students say they are considering taking the course next semester. I would say interest is picking up."

"Maybe I'll be lucky enough to have found a home then. I really do like the town and the people in it."

We talked a while longer before I left to go home. As soon as I pulled away from in front of Denise's house, I noticed a vehicle had fallen in behind me. As I went through town, I was able to identify the vehicle as a light-gray sedan about ten years old. The person driving was an amateur when it came to tailing somebody. He stuck so close to me that there was no question of him following me. The car pulled into the curb a couple of houses down from mine and killed his engine when I pulled into my driveway. I slipped out of my car, and using the blackness of the night, I started to work my way back to where the sedan had stopped. I worked my way past and to the back of the car. I cautiously stepped out into the street. I started to come up on the driver's side of the parked car.

Suddenly, the car engine roared to life. Before I could get to the car door, the driver sped off into the night with a squeal of tires. Too late, I realized there was a streetlight about a quarter of a block in back of me. The person in the car must have caught sight of me in their side mirror and decided to take off before I could get to them. Fortunately for them, their license plate light was burned out so I wasn't able to get their plate number.

Since my tail was long gone and I didn't expect him back anymore tonight, I returned home, took a shower, and turned in for the night.

Things were quiet for the next several days—no tails, no threats, no nothing, just life as usual.

Saturday I picked Denise up for an early dinner, and then we took in the show at the only theater in town. It was a show we both had been wanting to see. The evening was nice enough that I put the Caddy's top down before leaving from the theater. Arriving at Denise's house, we both got out of the car, as I was going to walk Denise to her door. We started up the walk, but before we got to the door, Amos Gains stepped out from behind a tree in Denise's yard. In his hand, he held a revolver, and he had it pointed right at us.

"Okay, you two, let's turn around and get right back in your car, Professor. The three of us are going for a little ride."

"What's this all about, Gains?" I asked.

"So you know who I am," he said, surprised.

"We've known about you ever since you had that meeting with Jack Finks a month or so ago at the cafe."

"Oh yes. Jack was always on the gutless side. He didn't like to be seen with me because of what people might think. We spent a little time together in jail. We would run into each other off and on like we did that day at the cafe. Now no more talk. Let's go."

"One last question. Why are you doing this? Neither one of us has ever done anything to you, and if it's robbery, just take what you want here."

"The reason for the ride is because neither one of you knows when to mind your own business. And don't think that by refusing to cooperate, I wouldn't do the job right here. Take my word on it that I will."

"At least tell us who wants us dead."

"Forget it. I never tell whom I work for. Now move."

"Hold it right there," the voice of Ben Hollister commanded from the darkness to our right. "Put the gun down nice and easy."

A wild, desperate look sprang into Amos's eyes. He started to swing his gun in the direction of Ben, who had stepped into the light of the streetlight. I sprang forward, hitting Amos's arm as he pulled the trigger. Ben returned fire. Amos and I went to the ground. I furiously struggled to control the arm and hand the gun was in. Slowly Amos brought the gun down between our bodies. Frantically, I held the barrel of the gun into Amos's body as I closed my finger on his trigger finger. Suddenly, the gun went off. I lay on top of Amos for a couple of seconds, waiting to feel some pain. When I didn't, I knew Amos was shot, not me.

"John! John! Are you all right?" Denise cried, running over to me. She grabbed me to help me up.

"Yeah, I'm fine. How about Ben?"

We hurried over to where Ben was on the ground. I opened his jacket. Blood was on his shirt, at his shoulder area. While Denise looked after Ben, I dialed 911 on my cell phone.

"Relax, Ben," Denise consoled him. "John is calling for an ambulance and backup now."

"911. What is your emergency, please?" the operator asked.

"I have a police officer wounded at 1040 Oak Street. I need police backup and an ambulance at this address."

"Is the officer conscious?"

"Yes, he is."

"Is he bleeding?"

"Yes. Not very bad, but some."

"The police and ambulance are on the way."

"Thank you."

Within five minutes, two patrol cars pulled up with sirens screaming. Two officers came rushing over, roughly pushing Denise aside. Sheriff Blocker pulled up in his car, got out, went over to Gains, and checked for a pulse. When he found one, he made sure Gains was secure and then came over to Ben.

"What happened, Ben?" he asked softly.

"I was on patrol when I saw suspicious activity on the grounds around Miss Cole's house here by the guy over there. I stopped to investigate, and that was when the professor and Miss Cole arrived. The guy covered the professor and Miss Cole with a gun and was attempting to kidnap them when I covered him with my weapon. The guy turned his gun on me and might have succeeded in killing me if the professor hadn't jumped on him, knocking his aim off. The professor and he struggled. The gun went off between them. Is the guy dead?"

"No. He's in real bad shape, but he's still alive."

"The professor was just trying to save his own life and Miss Cole's as well as mine."

The ambulance arrived then. They quickly loaded Ben up and, with sirens screaming, headed for the hospital.

"Are you okay, Professor?" the sheriff asked me.

"Yeah. I'm fine."

"And you, Miss Cole?"

"Thanks to Ben and John here, yes, I'm fine."

"Do either one of you know this guy?"

"No, but we both know of him. We know what his name is. We know what his rap sheet says about him. As far as ever meeting him face-to-face or talking to him, neither one of us ever has."

"What reason could he have had then for wanting to harm either one of you?"

"He was hired by someone else. I tried to get him to name who had hired him, but he wouldn't tell. I have my ideas on whom it might be, but nothing concrete. Just my own suspicions."

"Did he say why he was hired to come after you and Miss Cole?"

"Oh yes. He said we should have minded our own business. I can't speak for Denise here, but for myself, I'm just not built that way. I'll do whatever I can to help catch a crook."

"It doesn't surprise me that the maniac in town has you and Miss Cole in their crosshairs now," the sheriff said. "This is exactly what I was afraid would happen. The police are paid to run these risks, but private citizens aren't."

"All this guy has done is strengthen my resolve to bring him down. It makes me mad to have anybody threaten me or someone I care about. I will watch my back closer, though."

Just then, Martha returned home. When she saw the police cars, she rushed over to Denise.

"What in the world is going on here? Are you okay? What's with all the police, and who is that lying on the ground over there?"

"Relax, Mom. Everything is all right and under control. That guy lying there just wanted John and me to take a ride with him. John and I didn't want to, and when the guy insisted, John and he scuffled, with the guy over there coming out on the losing end. We are both okay. Let's go into the house, Mom. I'll see you later, John."

"Sure, Denise. Take care of your mother."

The second ambulance arrived to pick up Gains. He moaned as the ambulance crew carefully loaded him onto a gurney. The sheriff sent a deputy along with Gains in the ambulance since Gains was technically under arrest.

Amos passed in and out of consciousness all the way to the hospital. Upon arrival at the hospital, he was rushed into emergency surgery. Five hours later, he came out of surgery. He was still in critical but stable condition. A guard was posted outside his room.

It had been a long night for the deputy. Even though he knew he was due to be relieved in a couple of hours, he couldn't help but doze off. The sound of Gains's door closing abruptly woke him back up.

He jumped up off the chair and charged into the room. A guy in a white lab coat was by Gains's bed, looking at Gains's IV tubing. He quickly dropped the tubing.

"You're not the same doctor that has been taking care of this guy," the deputy said.

"Of course not, Officer. We had a shift change. I will be his doctor during this shift. Now I have other patients to attend to, so if you will excuse me…"

The deputy followed the doctor out of the room and sat back down. Shortly, the same doctor the deputy remembered as having attended Gains before appeared.

"I'll take one last look at your prisoner before I go off duty," he said to the deputy.

"One last look? The other doctor who was here a half hour ago said the shift was changing then."

"The shift is changing *now*. What was the other doctor's name?"

"I don't know. You guys all look alike to me in your white coats."
"What was the guy doing when you saw him here in the room?"

"He was by the bed, holding the IV tube in his hand. He dropped it when I came in."

"Did he have a syringe in his hand?"

"No."

The doctor looked the IV tubing over closely. Even though he wouldn't have been able to tell if anything had been injected into the line, everything looked okay. He examined Gains closely. Satisfied with his examination, he made a notation on Gains's chart.

"Dr. Shaffer will be your prisoner's doctor for the rest of the day."

Later that morning, I ran into Sheriff Blocker coming out of Ben's room as I was coming to see Ben.

"Good morning, Sheriff. How's Gains doing this morning?" "Still critical, but they got the bullet out okay."

"I'm glad he is still alive. I would personally much rather see him stand trial as opposed to me being instrumental in his demise."

"I'm glad you feel that way, Professor. I have to be on my way now. I need you to stop by the station sometime today to give me a statement on last night."

"Sure. Be happy to."

The sheriff left, and I went on in to see Ben. He was out of bed, sitting in the chair, looking out the window. A small smile creased his lips when he saw it was me who had come in. He looked drawn and fatigued from his wound.

"Good morning, Professor. Thank you for saving my life last night."

"One good turn deserves another. If it hadn't been for you, Denise and I might not still be kicking ourselves. How are you feeling this morning?"

"To be perfectly honest, it hurts like hell. I guess I'm just lucky I'm not in a bad a shape as the other guy is, or at least the sheriff said he is still in bad shape."

"Yeah, that's what he just told me too. Do you know when they are going to release you yet?"

"The doctor hasn't been around yet, so your guess is as good as mine. How is Denise?"

"She's fine. I haven't talked to her yet today, but she seemed fine when I left her last night. Do you have anybody to help you when you get home?"

"Yeah. I have a sister that lives in town. She has already told me she will stop by every day to do what I need help with."

"I suppose the sheriff will be relieving you of duty for a while."

"No. I'll be able to work inside the station on light duty until this heals."

"That's great, Ben. If there is anything I can do to help or just give you a hand with something that your sister can't handle, just give me a call."

"Thanks, John. I'll keep that in mind."

"I have to go now. I'm really glad you'll be okay, Ben."

I left the hospital to go to my car. Just as I exited the hospital, I saw the side profile of a man that I thought I recognized as that of Frank Duncan also going out to the parking lot. I couldn't think of any reason why he would be here. I knew Florence Duncan wasn't in the hospital because I had seen her coming out of the Administration Building just a day ago.

I hurried and tried to catch up to the man I thought was Frank. He was far enough ahead of me, though, that I lost sight of him for about ten seconds when he stepped on the other side of an RV. I sprinted to the RV and swept the area of the parking lot I hadn't been able to see before because of the RV blocking my view.

Three cars down, a man was just about to climb into a black Mercedes with darkly tinted windows, with the exception of the windshield. I could see now the man I thought was Frank Duncan sported a trimmed mustache and goatee. He was also wearing a pair of dark sunglasses. He hesitated for a second before sliding on into the car. I watched as he pulled out of the parking lot.

I had seen a black Mercedes just like that one in town before. Even though I knew I had seen the car around town, I had never seen who got in or out of it. I made up my mind I was going to try to get the plate number of the car the first chance I got.

Later that afternoon, Ben felt restless, so he wandered on down to Gains's room.

"Hi, Jim," Ben greeted the deputy on duty outside the room. "All quiet on the western front?"

"Oh yeah. Either this guy doesn't have family, or if he does, they don't care one way or another. There hasn't been anybody asking about him, come in to see him, or even call to see how he is doing."

"I pulled the rap sheet on this guy once. If I remember right, I don't think he does have any family. It doesn't surprise me either that nobody has asked about him. Neither did it surprise me when someone tried to kidnap them two people last night."

"It was them two professors from the college, wasn't it?"

"Yes, it was."

"Why in the world would anybody want to kidnap them?"

"I know they have both been poking around, trying to learn what they could about the rapes and murders that have been terrorizing the town. They have unearthed some revealing and interesting facts. Put yourself in this maniac's place. Would you want someone who could possible put you away in the pen for the rest of your life running around?"

"No, I guess I wouldn't. Do you think this guy here is the killer and rapist?"

"No, I don't. But we will be able to tell for sure once they get a DNA sample from this guy. They had gotten DNA samples of the rapist off the body he killed in the park."

"That would be great if he is. I've heard you know these two professors quite well."

"Her I've know now for about three years. Ever since she moved into town. As for him, I met him shortly after he moved here at the start of this semester. She is a great girl, and I might not be walking around yet if it hadn't been for him last night. Have you heard the doctors say how this guy is doing?"

"From what I've heard, he is still in critical condition. So far, he hasn't been conscious long enough at any one time for the sheriff to question him. I know the sheriff wants to talk to him real bad too."

"Is he in a coma?" Ben asked.

"Kind of, I guess. At any rate, he hasn't talked yet." Just then Ben's nurse appeared.

"Deputy Hollister," she said sternly, "you need to get back to your room. You need to rest."

While Ben was heading back to his room, I was busy making out a list of supplies that I needed to order. I got the list made out and took it over to the Maintenance Building to turn it in. As I stepped into the building, I came face-to-face with Florence Duncan on her way out.

"Good afternoon, Miss Duncan. How are you doing today?"

"Good afternoon, Professor Brennon. I'm doing fine. And you?"

"I'm doing fine also."

"I read in the paper this morning that Professor Cole and you had a bit of a harrying time last night. I'm glad the two of you are still with us," she said.

"It was touch and go for a little bit last night, but luckily, I came out on top. How is Frank doing?"

"Just fine. I'm so busy that I don't get a chance to see much of him. Sometimes a little bit at night."

"I thought I saw him at the hospital this morning. I was hoping there was nothing seriously wrong with him, if it was him. The guy I thought was Frank got away before I could get close enough to be certain if it was him or not."

"It couldn't have been Frank," she said positively. "There isn't anybody in the hospital right now that we know, and Frank's health is good. I'm sorry, but I really have to go now, Professor. It has been nice chatting with you."

"Do you know what kind of car Frank is driving?" I asked quickly.

"What kind of car he drives?" she repeated, caught by surprise.

"Yes. Do you know what kind of car he drives?" I asked again.

"Right now, I think he is driving a black Mercedes, but I'm not sure, because he rents whatever he drives. Sometimes he'll drive the same car for a few weeks, sometimes just for a few days. When he gets bored driving one car, he'll turn it in and rent something else. Now I really have to go. Goodbye."

The next morning, I had some spare time, so I decided to visit our local car rental company. I called Denise to see if she would like to accompany me on my quest if she had the time. She said she would love to, and she had the free time also. She was coming out of the Music Building when I pulled up to the curb. She sprinted on out to the car and slid in.

"Now why are we going to the car rental place? If you need to take your car into the garage, I will be happy to give you a ride wherever you need to go."

"No, I don't need to take the old girl into the garage, but we are going to see about me renting a black Mercedes."

"Oh. You don't like old Betsy here anymore?" she asked.

"Old Betsy and I are inseparable. I saw a guy get into a black Mercedes the other day when I had stopped at the hospital to see Ben and to find out how Gains was doing. At first, I thought the guy who got into the car was Frank Duncan, but when I got closer, I discovered the guy had a mustache and goatee."

"And if it was Duncan, them two things could have been fake," she pointed out.

"You're right on that count. I talked to Florence yesterday. I asked her what Frank drives. She said he is driving a black Mercedes at the present. She also said he always rents the cars he drives. I can't think of anyplace close, other than right here in town, where he would rent a car from—that is, if the place in town has luxury cars. But that is what I intend to find out."

"Here we are," Denise said.

I parked in front of a three-story building. A modest but very noticeable sign above the full glass doors read, "Thrifty Rentals." There wasn't a lot of vehicles parked around or at the back of the building. I assumed the top floor or maybe both floors were used for vehicle storage. The office was painted a cheerful light blue and eggshell white. A young pretty girl in her early twenties was standing behind a counter loaded with brochures.

"How may I be of service to you, sir?" she asked with a broad and sexy smile.

"To begin with, tell me what makes of cars Thrifty rents."

"We have a wide range of vehicles to choose from—from luxury to economy models. Which could I interest you in?"

"I'm real partial to black Mercedes."

"We do have a black Mercedes in our fleet. I will have to check and see if it's here or not. Please excuse me for a minute."

We watched as the clerk walked to the end of the counter and her computer. After a few keystrokes, she returned.

"I'm sorry, sir. That particular vehicle happens to be rented out at this time. We have several very nice Cadillacs and Lincolns on hand. May I interest you in one of them?"

"Now, dear, don't give the poor girl a hard time," Denise said. I looked closely at her for a second. I caught the sparkle in her eye and the sly smile on her lips. I knew her well enough by now that I realized she just felt like having a little fun. I decided to play along.

"But, honey, I had my heart set on a black Mercedes."

"Men can be such babies, can't they?" Denise said to the clerk.

"I'll tell you what, dear." She turned back to me. "We will split the difference between your Mercedes and a Volkswagen and settle on a Thunderbird."

"Or maybe this little lady here would be good enough to tell us who has that black Mercedes. Maybe I could talk that person into exchanging the car with another one. There could even be a bonus in it for you, ma'am, if the person turned it in soon, but I would need the person's name before I could talk to him or her."

"Are you trying to bribe this girl?"

"No. Not at all. I'm just trying to help her get another car rented, and then by calling me, she will still have the Mercedes rented."

The clerk said, "As tempting as your offer is, sir, I can't give out the names of our customers unless you are a police officer, and then I would need to see some identification."

"Either get something else, dear, or let's be on our way," Denise chided me.

"You take all the fun out of car shopping. Okay, I'll go quietly, but if you call me, ma'am, when that Mercedes is available, I would really appreciate it. Here is my name and number."

"I will certainly give you a call when the car is available… Mr. Brennon," the clerk said.

We bid the clerk goodbye and retreated to outside. We burst out laughing when we got into the car.

"I haven't had fun like that in quite some time," she said.

"You played the part perfectly. For a minute, I thought I had my ex-wife in there with me."

"Is that good or bad?"

"Oh, she wasn't all bad. We each had our good and bad days. Too many people try to shove all the blame on the other person when a marriage doesn't work out. Neither party is entirely at fault or entirely faultless. I learned a whole lot from my first marriage. Hopefully, I won't make the same mistakes the second time around, if there is a second time."

"I've stayed out of that trap so far. Not that I don't think marriage can be great because I know it can be. My mom and dad had a great marriage. The whole trouble comes in trying to find the right partner. I've seen too many high school friends get married and then, in a relatively short period of time, split because they found out they couldn't stand the sight of each other. I'll wait."

"What about kids? I thought all women wanted kids."

"I can take them or leave them. I don't have any great burning desire to have a house full of them. Did you have any with your first wife?"

"No. She never could get pregnant, which in the end was a good thing."

"Well, back to our black Mercedes. Do you think our friend Frank Duncan is the guy driving Thrifty's Mercedes?" she asked.

"Yes, I do. I also think it was him I saw at the hospital. The only question is, why was he there, or whom had he seen in the hospital?"

We went back to the college, and I dropped Denise off in front of the Music Building. Since I had a class that afternoon, I grabbed an early lunch then went to the classroom to prepare for the afternoon class.

All day long, the halls of the hospital was filled with doctors, nurses, and visitors. Toward evening, the flow started to dwindle as the doctors finished up their operations for the day. Nurses were getting their patients settled in for the evening since dinner had been served and the trays collected and sent back down to the kitchen.

Around nine o'clock, the nurses dimmed the hall lights so the patients that wanted their doors open could see a little of what was going on outside their rooms but could also relax and go to sleep if they wanted to without a bright light shining into their room. Most of the lights in the rooms were also turned low.

In Amos Gains's room, there was just the one wall light on above the head of his bed. Amos moved his head from side to side in slow motion as he tried to regain consciousness.

Outside the door, the deputy had to go to the restroom. Since the public restroom was down the hall a very short distance away, the deputy figured he could go to the restroom, do what he had to do, and be back at his post all within a couple of minutes.

As the deputy trotted toward the restroom, a tall white-coated man smoothly slipped into Gains's room. The only sound in the room was the regular *beep, beep, beep* of his heart monitor machine. The white-coated man moved to the side of Amos's bed.

Amos's eyes fluttered for a couple of seconds before focusing in on who was standing over him. Amos smiled until he saw the syringe in his visitor's hand. His eyes flashed between the man's face and the syringe. Fear spread across Amos's face.

"What…what are you going to do?" he asked, terrified.

"I'm just going to give you something that will put you to sleep and wipe away all your problems."

"Please…please…I haven't said a word to the cops or anybody else. I promise, no matter what the cops do, I won't talk."

"Now, Amos, that is what you say now, but if they offered you a deal and you were to turn state's evidence and they put you in the Witness Protection Program, you would be able to live pretty good without having to do a lick of work. And I know you don't like to work. You can understand why I really can't take a chance of that happening, right?"

The man stuck the needle of the syringe into the IV tubing at the place provided. He started to push the plunger down.

"Help!" Amos weakly cried out as panic filled him.

"Now don't cause a ruckus, Amos," the man said softly. He quickly clamped a hand over Amos's mouth before Amos could get out a second cry for help. Amos weakly struggled. "Just relax. It will all be over in a minute."

He finished emptying the syringe into the IV. Amos's struggles became weaker and then stopped entirely. The steady beeps of the monitor became irregular. Then the beeps ceased, and the machine made one steady sound. Amos's heart had stopped beating.

Within a few seconds, there came the call of code red over the public address system. When the crash cart team burst into the room, the man appeared to be doing CPR on Gains. He stepped back and out of the way of the crash cart personnel. As they started to work on Gains, the killer moved to the door and slipped out of the room. The drama unfolding at the bed held the deputy's attention, so he didn't notice the white-coated figure slip out of the room. Moving swiftly but not hurriedly, the killer vacated the hospital in ten minutes' time.

Back in Gains's room, the doctor who had arrived with the crash cart pronounced Gains dead after doing everything he could to revive him.

The sheriff was called after Gains was pronounced dead. He told the deputy to stay on duty outside the room and not to let anybody in the room until he got there.

Fifteen minutes later, Sheriff Blocker came striding down the hall. The deputy followed the sheriff into Gains's room. Blocker looked the room over first. When he didn't find anything, he switched his attention to the dead body of Gains. He paid particular attention to Gains's mouth. Finally, he motioned for the deputy to follow him out into the hall.

He arranged for the local funeral home to pick up the body and hold it overnight before sending it to Lincoln the following day for possible toxicology tests and an autopsy. As the sheriff and deputy were preparing to go to a conference room, the doctor that pronounced Gains dead stopped at the nurse's station.

"Excuse me, Doctor," Sheriff Blocker said to him. "Could I see you for a minute?"

"Certainly." The doctor followed the sheriff and deputy into the conference room. "What can I do for you?" he asked after everybody got seated.

"What was Gains's current condition before he died?"

"He was still in very serious condition, but he had improved during the day today."

"Did he ever regain consciousness?"

"Not that I know of, but he had improved enough that we felt that the possibility of him waking up at any time was strong."

"Okay, Doc. That is all I'll need from you. Thank you for your time."

"Anytime, Sheriff."

"Okay, Deputy Hays," the sheriff said, turning to the uncomfortable deputy after the doctor left. "Suppose you tell me exactly what happened here tonight."

"I really don't know. Nobody went in that room unless I went in with them. I've lost count of how many doctors and nurses have been in that room since I came on duty."

"You never had to leave your post here in the hall for any reason at all? Not even for a minute or two?"

"Well, just before he died, I did have to go to the restroom. The restroom is just a few steps down the hall, and I was only gone for two minutes at the very most. I didn't have any choice. I had to go. I didn't think anything could happen in that short a time."

"Now you know it can. It's water under the bridge now, though. It just took a second for someone to duck into the room while you were gone. When you came back from the restroom, you didn't hear any sounds coming from inside the room?"

"No, sir. I hadn't been back no more than five minutes before I heard the code red call for this room over the PA. The next thing I knew, a crash cart crew came tearing down the hall. They stormed into the room and started to try to revive Gains."

"Now think carefully. Was the room empty when the crash cart entered the room?"

"Well, yes…it must have been," Deputy Hays said uncertainly. "The nurses went in first. Then the doctor went in with me, bringing up the rear." A perplexed look came on his face then. "That can't be right, because there was a doctor already giving CPR to Gains when the nurses reached the bed. The first doctor stepped back then to give the crash cart people room to work. I didn't give the first doctor a second thought."

"Did this other doctor that was doing the CPR stay in the room as the crash cart team tried to revive Gains?"

"I don't think so. I was watching them trying to revive Gains, and I lost track of him in the excitement. I'm sorry, Sheriff."

"Can you give me a description of this other doctor?"

"No. There was so much activity in the room. I can't describe anybody who was in the room."

"That is too bad, Deputy, because I think the guy that got away killed Gains in cold blood."

"I don't understand. When I saw him, he was doing CPR on Gains. Why would he try to save Gains if he had just killed?"

"Think about it. What better way of making your escape than to blend in so nobody really would remember you? Plus, there were bruises on both sides of Gains's mouth, which means Gains must have regained consciousness and tried to call out for help when he realized he was about to be killed. Only our killer was able to put his hand over Gains's mouth to stop him before he could cry out. And as far as why he killed Gains? Gains could identify him, and he wasn't going to take that chance."

"What crime could Gains identify him for?"

"Gains admitted to Professor Brennon that he was hired to kidnap and kill Miss Cole and him. When that plan fell through, our killer decided to eliminate one of the risks to his safety."

"What are your orders for me now that he isn't here for me to guard any longer?"

"By the time you get back to the station, it will be time for you to go off duty. Go back on patrol tomorrow. I'll finish up here."

It took a couple of days before the paper got wind of Gains's death. When it did find out, the news was splashed all over the front page. I carefully read the entire story. The Sheriff's Office told the paper Gains had died from unknown causes. The press release did mention that the cause of death could have been from complications of the injuries he had suffered during his recent kidnapping attempt.

I knew Ben would be off today since it was Sunday. I had intended to go over to Ben's house anyhow to find out how he was doing and see if he needed anything I could help him with. I jumped in my car and went over to Ben's house. He answered the doorbell right away.

"How are you doing, Ben?" I asked as we went into the living room and got seated.

"Pretty good, John. They keep me busy down at the station." "Have you seen the paper this morning yet?"

"Oh yeah. I assume you are referring to the headlines on the front page?"

"Yep. Was the cause of death really complications, or was it something more sinister, like murder, and the complication line was just a smoke screen Sheriff Blocker threw to the press?"

"What makes you think Gains was killed? People die from complications all the time."

"For one thing, the morning after the attack, when I visited you in the hospital, Gains was in critical condition, all right, but he was still alive. He was still alive two days later. Then suddenly, he dies? I'm no expert, but from what I know about gunshot wounds—and I do know a little—the majority of the time, the victim only lasts a little while before dying of their wounds, if that is what they die from."

"You really should have been a cop, John. We won't know for sure until the autopsy comes back. Sheriff Blocker also ordered a toxicology scan done on Gains. He thinks Gains might have been killed with some type of poison."

"And nobody out of the ordinary was seen on the flour or anywhere near his room during the evening?"

"The rumor around the station is that Deputy Hays, who was on duty at the time, had to go to the restroom and someone slipped into the room while he was gone and did the job on Gains."

"This guy has to be stopped. He's racking up just way too many victims. So far, he's been too smart to leave hardly any clues behind. Of course, I wasn't around yet when the first rapes occurred, so I don't know what clues the sheriff picked up from them crimes."

"This is what has been the police department's problem—no good clues and no eyewitnesses. We've gotten DNA evidence off the victims, but unfortunately, it's not doing any good until we can arrest somebody and match up the DNA we have with theirs," Ben said, shaking his head.

"We just need a way of luring him into doing something that would be incriminating. Has the police department ever tried a sting operation?"

"No. We only have two women on the force. Sheriff Blocker has always felt the culprit was someone local so they would recognize our female officers instantly and wouldn't bite. It's a great idea, and I think the sheriff would be interested in trying it if we had a new officer on the force that wouldn't be recognized instantly."

"Has the sheriff ever asked the state police if he could use one of their female officers for a sting operation?"

"I don't know if he ever thought of using the state police for a sting operation or not. I could bring the idea up tomorrow. Sheriff Blocker will always listen to suggestions, and if he likes what is suggested, he has acted on them before."

"Ben, could you possibly give me a call and kind of tell me basically what the autopsy report says and maybe tell me what really killed Gains? I would really appreciate it."

"I think I can do that, John. It will be several days before we get the reports, but I'll give you a call when we do."

"Okay, Ben. Before I take off, is there anything I can do for you?"

"No. Thanks anyhow. Take care, and I'll talk to you in a few days."

CHAPTER

TEN

The next day, after a morning of filing reports, filing police copies of tickets written, and doing general police station work, Ben knocked on Sheriff Blocker's office door. He told Ben to come in.

"What is it, Deputy Hollister?"

"I have a suggestion I would like to make, sir."

"Sure. What is the suggestion?"

"Yesterday John Brennon came by to see me. In the course of our conversation, he asked if we had ever tried a sting operation to catch the rapist and killer. I mentioned there were only two women on the force so the killer would probably recognize them right off the bat. He thought maybe if we asked the state police to loan us one of their female officers, maybe the killer could be lured into attacking her."

"Okay, Hollister. I'll give the suggestion some serious thought. Is there anything else?"

"No, sir."

After Ben left, the sheriff thought about a sting operation. It just might work if he could get the state police to loan him an officer. He knew a captain in the state police. They had been friends since high school. He also knew the phone number of the captain. The phone rang a half a dozen times before it was answered.

"Captain Springfield."

"Rick, this is Walt Blocker. How are things going for you?"

"Walt! It's good to hear from you. Things are going pretty good on my end. Janet sends her love. What's up on your end?"

"I don't know if you've heard anything about the trouble I've been having here in Cedar Falls or not."

"Can't say that I have. Sorry."

"What it amounts to, Rick, is that in the last four months, I have had four rapes, three murders, one attempted rape, and one dead dog thrown in for good measure. I'm convinced all these crimes were committed by the same maniac. The main problem I'm having is that this guy is no dummy. I really don't have any firm suspects."

"I'm sorry you're having so many problems, Walt. Word hasn't trickled down to us in Lincoln yet. Were you calling because there was something the state police could help you with?"

"One of my deputies suggested doing a sting operation to try to lure this pervert into revealing himself. I have considered that option before, but we only have two women on our force. They would be recognized instantly. I was wondering if it would be possible for me to borrow one of your female officers to run a sting operation here? If I could get her for a few days or, at the longest, for a week, it would really help me out."

"Let me check with my superiors, but I will do everything in my power to get you one or two officers to help you. Give me, let's say, a couple or three hours to get back to you."

"Thanks a lot, Rick. I appreciate anything you and the state police can do for me. Talk to you later."

Sheriff Blocker spent the next couple of hours making plans for the sting operation in the event he could get the female officer he had requested. Three hours later, the phone rang. Captain Springfield was on the other end.

"I explained your situation to my superiors, and they could see what your problem is. They gave me the green light to ask for a volunteer to be your bait. We have several officers who has worked on sting operations of this nature before. I selected the one I thought would be best for you and asked her if she would be interested in taking an assignment to work a sting operation in Cedar Falls for no longer than a week. She said she would. Her name is Officer Mary Dean. She will report to you for duty Wednesday morning."

"Thanks a lot, Rick. The whole town has been terrorized for several months now, and I desperately need to put this guy away."

"Well, I hope you catch this guy. Officer Dean will do her part. Take care, and give me a call soon. Bye for now."

Sheriff Blocker stepped out into the station's front area. There was somebody at the counter, asking a question about parking a trailer. As soon as the officer answered the guy's question and had left, the sheriff called for everybody's attention.

"I want every officer in the main conference room. Hays, stay at the counter. Somebody can tell you what it's all about later."

Everybody filed into the conference room and grabbed a seat. The murmur of voices subsided and then stopped when the sheriff went to the head of the table.

"I called the state police. They have agreed to send an officer to Cedar Falls to assist us in running a sting operation. She will be here Wednesday morning. I have a plan figured out, and this officer has agreed to be the bait. We will have the services of the officer for one week. Since all the rapes have happened at night, that is when we will put the operation in motion. I just wanted everybody to be up to date on what's happening. The members of the force that will actually be participating in the operation will receive their assignments when I brief the whole team, which will include the new officer. I will post on the bulletin board tomorrow who will make up the team. That will be all for now. Thank you."

The next day, Ben waited impatiently for the sheriff to post who would make up the operation team. Finally, the sheriff posted what Ben hoped was the list of team members on the bulletin board. As soon as the sheriff disappeared back into his office, Ben, as well as a couple of other officers who happened to be in the room, rushed over to the bulletin board. Ben saw his name was on the list.

Later that afternoon, the autopsy and toxicology reports on Gains came across his desk to be filed. Before filing them, though, he carefully read them. It was as the sheriff had suspected. Gains had been poisoned. The poison used was cyanide. Ben racked his brain, trying to figure out where a person could get their hands on cyanide. Then he remembered what a girl he had dated at one time had told him.

She was taking a chemistry course at the college at the time. She had mentioned how if a person wanted to get their hands on just about any poison, they wouldn't have any trouble finding it in the chemistry department inventory.

John could probably find out for me easily if the chemistry department has any cyanide, Ben thought.

After Ben got off duty, he swung around to my house. He didn't see my car in the driveway because I had driven it into the garage and closed the door. He took a chance that I might be home anyhow and rang the front doorbell.

"Ben! Come in. Come in," I said, holding the door open for him. "Can I interest you in a cold beer or Coke?"

"I'm off duty, so a cold beer would taste real good."

"Have a seat, and I'll get you that cold one. As a matter of fact, I'll join you in a cold one."

I went over to the wet bar and grabbed a couple of beers out of the refrigerator nestled under the bar. I took them over to where Ben had settled himself on the couch. We both took a pull on our beers and got comfortable.

"To what do I owe the pleasure of your visit? Not that you need a reason," I added hastily.

"Two things, really. One, I suggested to Sheriff Blocker that sting operation you and I had talked about. He liked the idea, and he got lucky with the state police. They have loaned us a female cop for a week. Hopefully, that will be long enough to lure the rapist out into the open."

"When will she be here?"

"Tomorrow morning. The sheriff has already made up a team. I happen to have been chosen to be on the team."

"So the sheriff will probably start running the operation tomorrow night."

"I would imagine he will. Also, the autopsy and toxicology reports on Gains came in today."

"Yeah?" I said eagerly, leaning forward in my chair.

"It was just as Sheriff Blocker thought. Gains had been poisoned with cyanide. Now I need a favor from you."

"Anything, Ben. Just name it."

"At one time, I dated a girl who was taking a chemistry course at the college. She told me the chemistry department had poisons galore in their inventory. Could you find out if that inventory includes cyanide?"

"I shouldn't have any trouble finding that out for you. I'll check tomorrow morning and give you a call at the station. Do you carry a cell phone, Ben?"

"Yes."

"Do you normally have it turned on?"

"Yes. Why are you so interested in whether I normally carry a cell phone and if I have it on, John?"

"As you know, I've been threatened a couple of times. Gains tried to kidnap Denise and me, and I have no doubt that he fully intends to kill both of us. I hope you understand that it would just make me feel a little safer if I was able to call somebody for help no matter where I am. If you don't want to give me your number, I understand, Ben."

"No, no, that's okay. I don't mind giving it to you, and if you need to call me, don't hesitate to do so. Here, I'll write it down for you."

He wrote his number down for me and handed me the slip of paper. We talked a while longer before Ben got up to leave. I walked him to the door. After Ben left, I went back into the living room and sat down. I thought about what Ben had told me about the sting operation they were going to run. I gradually formulated a plan of my own in my mind. After I was satisfied with what I had come up with, I relaxed with a book for a while before taking a shower and hitting the sack.

A very pretty woman who looked to be about thirty years of age and five feet, six inches tall; had shoulder-length blond hair and a very well-proportioned body; and dressed in a tight but not overly tight sweater, knee-length tight skirt, and moderate high- heeled shoes walked into the police station. The eyes of every male officer in the station instantly focused on her.

"May I see Sheriff Blocker, please?" she asked with a sexy voice.

"Oh…y-yes. Please…this way," Deputy Hays said nervously.

He led the woman to Sheriff Blocker's office and knocked. "Come in."

"There is a lady to see you, sir," he said after poking his head into the sheriff's office.

"Show her in."

Deputy Hays opened the door, and the lady stepped into the office, closing the door behind her.

"Please have a seat, ma'am. What can I do for you?"

"Thank you. I'm Officer Mary Dean from the state police, reporting for duty."

"Welcome to Cedar Falls, Officer Dean. I must say I'm surprised not to see you in uniform."

"I have a special reason for not wearing my uniform. Captain Springfield briefed me on what your situation is here in Cedar Falls. Since the perpetrator could very well be a local person, I didn't want to advertise my presence here as a cop. I've gone into other towns the same size as Cedar Falls to help with sting operations. It has always produced the fastest results when I hit town wearing regular clothes."

"It makes perfect sense. If you would like to get settled in at the motel down the street, I can have the team assembled here at the station at two o'clock. We'll go over tonight's operation then."

"That's fine, Sheriff. I'll be back at two. And you said the motel is right down the street?"

"Yes. When you leave the station, go to your right. It's five or six blocks down."

"Thank you."

At the same time Officer Dean was leaving the police station, I was getting out of a cab in front of Thrifty Car Rentals. The girl behind the counter was the same one on duty when Denise and I had come in before. She recognized me as I stepped in the door. "I'm very sorry, sir, but that black Mercedes hasn't been turned in yet," she apologized.

"That's okay. My wife convinced me to rent a dark-colored Ford or Chevy. What have you got in stock along those lines?"

"Let me look real fast," she said, moving down to the end of the counter and to her computer. I followed. "Well, it looks like I could fix you up with a dark-green Ford. Would that work for you?"

"That will be fine. I'll take it."

"Okay. I'll need to see your driver's license. Will you be needing insurance from us, or do you have your own?"

"I have my own."

"And do you know how long you will be needing the car, sir?"

"Probably no longer than a week."

"Okay. If you would be good enough to sign this right down here, I'll have your car brought around to the front. And will the deposit be cash, check, or credit card?"

"Cash."

"That will be one hundred dollars, sir."

By the time I paid the deposit and signed the rental agreement, the car had been brought around to the front. I thanked the girl behind the counter and went out to the car. I missed the feel of the Cadillac's wheel in my hands as I drove the Ford back to the college.

I checked the campus map and located the building that housed the Chemistry Department. I parked and went into the building, hoping the main lab would be marked. None was marked, so I stopped a student and asked him which one was the main lab. He pointed it out to me, and I went on in.

Some of the less dangerous chemicals were sitting out at the different workstations. The more dangerous chemicals were locked up in cabinets. Wire mesh reinforced the glass in the doors. I did my best to look at the contents of one cabinet.

"Who are you, and what are you doing in this lab?" a man's stern voice demanded from behind me.

I turned to find a college security guard standing there. "I'm Professor Brennon. I was just looking while waiting for a chemistry professor to show up."

"I don't recognize your name, and I've worked here at the college now for ten years. I know about every professor here at the college. You said you were just looking. Looking for what?"

"Nothing. I'll come back when I can talk to one of the chemistry professors."

I started to move toward the door to leave. The guard cut me off, preventing me from leaving.

"Hold on just a second, sir. Please stand over there while I take a quick look around."

The guard kept one eye on me while he looked over the cabinet that I had been standing in front of. He then moved down the bank of cabinets. He stopped in front of one and looked at it closer. I was surprised when the guard took a pen out of his pocket and opened the cabinet door. He drew his gun then and covered me with it.

"Up against the wall! Don't give me any trouble." I faced the wall.

"This is Brown in chemistry lab 121. A cabinet has been broken into. I have a guy in custody who says his name is Brennon. He claims to be a professor here. I'll hold him for Mr. Scott," he said into his radio.

He patted me down while we waited for the department head to show up. Soon a distinguished-looking older man strode into the room.

"I was told a cabinet had been broken into. You must be Brennon?" he asked, indicating me.

"Yes, I am. Professor Cole can vouch for who I am."

"I believe you. I've heard about the new Astronomy Department, and I've seen you around campus. I figured since you were new and the Astronomy Department is new, you had to be the new professor on campus."

"Thank you for giving me the benefit of the doubt. It's too bad there isn't any way of being able to tell when this was broken into," I said.

"It has happened within the last two weeks. Prior to that, there was work being done in the lab. The construction was completed two weeks ago. There has been classes held in this lab since."

"Maybe one of the workmen broke into the cabinet? People abuse so many different substances that maybe someone saw something that could be sold for the drug value of it or something that could be used for the manufacture of one of the more popular drugs."

"I doubt it," Scott said, dismissing the idea. "Given the sensitivity of the materials in the lab, college security was present whenever they were working in here."

"So the break-in had to have taken place sometime during the last two weeks and, more than likely, at night when the building would be deserted, except for when the guards made their rounds."

"I would say that is the correct hypothesis. Now let's take a look at that cabinet."

The three of us walked over to the cabinet. The lock was scratched, probably from a pick. It looked like that didn't work, so it was finally just pried open. Scott looked through the jars of chemicals. Then he looked through them again in a more hurried fashion.

"Are you missing something?" I asked.

"Well, yes, I am," he said in a distraught voice.

"And would that possibly be cyanide you're missing?" I asked. Scott jumped like he had been shot.

"Why would you ask that?" he demanded.

"I'm right, am I not?" I pressed.

"Yes," he reluctantly admitted. "I'm extremely upset because this is the first time that I know of that anything had ever been stolen out of this department. And since cyanide is a very potent poison, it worries me why someone would steal it. The obvious reason makes me sick." Suddenly, he turned to the guard. "Mr. Brown, did you search the good professor very thoroughly?"

"Yes, sir, I did. He never left my sight from the time I first saw him in here until when I searched him. I found nothing on him, and he certainly didn't have the time or opportunity to dispose of anything."

"I apologize, Professor Brennon, but I hope you understand I had to ask."

"I understand how you feel, and I would react the very same way if I was in your place. It's your department, but if I were you, I would probably keep the lab locked up at all times. It was wide open when I walked in."

"That is a very good suggestion and one I will give serious thought to. Now I had better report this to the police."

The three of us left the room, with Scott locking the lab door behind us. I was close to the Music Building, so I decided to take a chance of catching Denise in her office. I knocked on her office door and was happy to hear her tell me to come in.

"Hello, John. How is everything going?"

"I think I know where the guy that killed Gains in the hospital got his cyanide from to do the job," I said, sitting down.

"And where would that be?"

"I just came from the main chemistry laboratory. One of the cabinets that housed the more volatile chemicals had been broken into. As far as Scott, the department head—I'm sure you already knew his name— could tell, the only thing missing was a small quantity of cyanide. Now the question is, Who all knew there was even cyanide in that lab? The only people I can think of would be a chemistry professor, maybe the spouse of a professor, or a student. Since Gains was killed with cyanide, I would say this theft and his death are connected. What do you think?"

"I would say it's a very, very good possibility. Was anybody able to figure out when the cabinet was broken into?"

"Sometime within the last two-week period. Nice that Scott could narrow it down that close," I said sarcastically.

"I suppose it will be reported to the police, won't it?"

"Scott said he was going to report it. To me, what's so ominous about all this is that the theft and the death of Gains both happened in the same time frame. Since cyanide isn't something you can just pick up anyplace, it had to be the killer who broke into the lab."

"I gather this was all just discovered today."

"You got it."

"I'm curious. What were you doing in the chemistry lab? You never mentioned having an interest in chemistry before. Or is that where you meet your girlfriends?" she joked.

"Oh no. When it comes to girlfriends, I'm Diamond Jim. The sky is the limit for whoever happens to be the lucky lady at the time," I replied, laughing. "Seriously, the reason I was there was because Ben had asked me if I would check and see if our chemistry department had cyanide in their inventory. I can't think of any reason for the department to have cyanide in their inventory, but then I'm no chemist either." I looked at my watch. "Oh, I'm sorry to have to run, but it's getting a little late. I have to grab a bite to eat before dark."

"You sound like a man that has something to do or someplace to go," she said.

"Well, yes, there was something I had planned on doing tonight," I said hesitantly.

"Okay. I was going to invite you to dinner after I finished up here. My treat. Mom is going to be gone for the evening, so I thought we might have dinner together. But I understand if you have other plans."

"I'd love to have dinner with you, Denise. It's just that, well, tonight the police is going to run their first sting operation with the state police officer. I kind of intend on 'joining' the surveillance team. I want to be there to see this guy caught in the worst way."

"Our cops, at least some of them—Ben, for sure—will recognize your car instantly. And I wouldn't put it past Blocker to have you arrested for obstructing justice. You would just be getting yourself in trouble if you do this, John."

"You are probably right except for one thing. I won't be driving the Cadillac. I'll be driving a dark-green Ford."

"You've already got this other car, don't you?"

"Yeah. I rented it just before I went to the chemistry lab and then over here."

"Wouldn't you like to have some company on your stakeout?"

"It could be dangerous, Denise. I could never forgive myself if anything happened to you."

"How much danger could we possible be in? There are going to be cops watching everything that will happen. If this pervert shows his face, the cops will grab him fast. So let me come along."

"Well, I guess you have a valid point about the danger aspect of it. I guess it wouldn't hurt for you to come."

"Do you know where they are going to set up?" she asked.

"No. I figured all I have to do is park close enough to the police station so I can see when the sheriff and Ben, along with the new cop, come out. Then I will follow them—at a discreet distance, of course—to where they will set up."

"What with Cedar Falls being as small as it is, where do you think they will set up?"

"My guess is, Blocker will pick one of the spots the guy had used before. If I were to pick a spot, I'd go back to the park. It gives the killer a little cover, and even though there is some lighting in the park, there is still plenty of shadows for the killer to use to his advantage."

"Okay. I'll be done here in ten minutes, and then we can grab a quick bite to eat and then go on the stakeout."

I sat and contemplated Denise as I waited. She would make someone a very good wife someday.

Fire and lust stirred in the breast of the man sitting in his apartment. It had been a while since he had been able to satisfy his burning desires. He thought about the last time he had satisfied himself in the park. He might not have killed her if she hadn't fought him. But then, he thought with a satanic smile, he enjoyed cutting their throats so much.

It was dusk when, carrying an overnight bag, he walked into the park, which was at present deserted. He looked around a little and decided to lie in hiding back in the bushes he had used last time. He got among the bushes and quickly changed from a print shirt and tan slacks into his all-black outfit. He settled down to wait, hoping that some young well-built girl would stroll within his greedy reach. He knew girls had stopped walking in the park by themselves for a while, but slowly they were coming back. He hoped tonight one would decide it would be safe to walk through the park.

When Denise finished her tasks, and we left the Music Building. We stopped at Jim's Cafe to grab a hamburger. We then stationed ourselves half a block down the street from the police station. Just before darkness fell, Sheriff Blocker, Ben, three other officers, and a woman we had never seen before, which had to be the officer from the state police, exited the police station and got into several different cars. Denise and I followed the caravan to the park.

The state police officer got out of the sheriff's car and strode into the park. Two officers carefully followed the policewoman into the park and fanned out. The short hairs stood up on the back of Officer Dean's neck as she walked through the park. This only happened during an operation like this when someone other than fellow officers were watching her. The feeling intensified as she walked deeper into the park.

The eyes of the man in black hungrily watched every step her mini skirted legs took. He crouched, getting ready to spring, waiting for her to get a little closer to the bushes he was hiding in. Steadily she approached the area where the killer lay in wait.

Just as she was about to pass it, he sprang. He wrapped his arm around her neck and pulled her to the ground. She rolled with him and slipped out of his grip. They both sprang to their feet and faced each other. Just then, the two officers that had been shadowing Officer Dean stepped out with their guns drawn.

"Stop! Hands in the air!" they ordered.

Without a second's hesitation, the killer dove back into the bushes. Officer Dean sprang into the bushes after him after a second's hesitation. That second was a second too late. Wearing the cloak of darkness over his black outfit, he skillfully sped through the park toward what seemed to be an impenetrable row of bushes. With a desperate surge, he threw himself through the bushes.

The sheriff had stationed Ben and himself at the park entrance. Ben was closest to where the killer broke through.

"Halt!" Ben shouted.

When the fugitive didn't stop, Ben opened fire on him. The fugitive didn't seem to break stride as he raced away from the park and out into the night.

Denise and I were sitting in my rental car, watching the sheriff and Ben, when a black shape crashed through the bushes almost opposite of our car, which was parked on the far side of the street. We heard the report of Ben's gun when he fired. The black-clad figure seemed to falter for just a step or two before the night swallowed him.

I pulled away from the curb, went up to the next intersection, and turned the corner. I turned around in the first driveway I came to. I drove back down to the street bordering the park and drove in the direction the black-clad figure had taken off in. As I drove past the spot where the guy had smashed through the bushes, we saw the sheriff and Ben going over the sidewalk with flashlights, probably looking for blood to verify if Ben's shot had hit the guy.

Denise and I slowly cruised the streets, hoping we would catch a glimpse of the guy in black.

"Well, you and the sheriff were both right as to where to try the sting," Denise complimented me. "Since they didn't catch the guy, even though they had their chance, I doubt if they would have any luck with another try, at least in the park. I can't believe they let him escape."

"Wait a minute. I thought I saw something move up there in the shadows," I said, pointing.

We both strained our eyes, looking into the shadows of the houses, trees, and other things. Then we saw a dark shape separate from one shadow and blend almost instantly within another shadow. Since I had been driving with my lights off, all I could hope for was that whomever we were watching was the suspect and that he might not take notice of us. It was hard to keep track of him because there were intervals of five to ten minutes before he would move.

Finally, after a half hour or more of tailing him, we saw him enter a two-story apartment building. I hoped he would go into one of the two apartments on the ground floor, but instead he started to climb the stairs to the second floor. I kept hoping he would turn his uncovered head so we could get a look at him, but he never did. He favored his one leg as he climbed the stairs. The lights were on in both of the second-floor apartments. We had no way of knowing which apartment our man had gone into.

"What do you think we ought to do, John? Go back and get the sheriff? If we describe how this guy is dressed, I'm sure the sheriff would agree this is probably the guy they have been after."

"Oh, I'm sure he would. The problem is, if we go back to get the sheriff, he would probably already be gone from the park. By the time we run him down, tell him our story, and have him back here, this guy might already be long gone. I don't think he is going to stay long."

"Or you could keep watch here. I'll take the car and go back after the sheriff. Just don't try and be a hero while I'm gone."

"I'll have to try to stop him if he tries to leave. He has gotten away too many times. It's time he is stopped."

"If it comes to that, just be as careful as you can."

We both got out of the car. She slid behind the wheel and took off while I melted into the shadows to keep watch.

The man in black heard the command to halt as soon as he burst through the bushes.

They are crazy if they think I'm going to meekly give myself up, he said to himself.

He took one step to flee in the opposite direction when he heard the report of the shot Ben fired. A burning fire in his thigh made him falter for a step or two. He then ignored the pain in his leg as he again escaped into the suburban jungle. A previous short training period in the practice of camouflage and concealment enabled him to slowly move from shadow to shadow with the minimum amount of time in the moonlight. He didn't notice the dark-green Ford pacing his every move.

He took one last look around before breaking his cover and going into the apartment building. He hurried up the stairs as fast as his wounded leg would let him. He let himself into his apartment and carefully locked the door behind him.

He went into the bathroom and stripped his black shirt off. He then untied the pressure bandage he had made from a black T-shirt someone had placed on a clothesline in a backyard he had passed. The blood started to flow down his leg again. Quickly he took his black pants off and tossed them aside.

His wound really didn't look too bad. The bullet had gone straight through his thigh. The bleeding had slowed down, but it looked like the wound was going to need some stitching. He certainly couldn't go to the hospital here in town, and he didn't feel comfortable going to Lincoln. But there was a doctor in a small town about twenty miles away that would sew him up without asking a lot of questions, especially if the money pot was sweet enough.

He put a pressure bandage back on the wound and quickly got dressed with clothes that he kept in the apartment. It was when he was putting the bloody pants into a black garbage bag that he suddenly realized he had left his overnight bag in the park with the clothes in it that he had worn to the park. It was a mistake but one he really couldn't have helped making. With cops all over the place, he was lucky he got away at all. Even if the police traced the clothing or bag back to this apartment somehow, they wouldn't discover his name because he had rented it under a fictitious name.

He was at the door, ready to open it, when he saw the knob slowly turning. He pulled a blackjack out of his pant's back pocket and positioned himself so he would be behind the door when it was opened.

I watched the apartment building, waiting for Denise to get back with the sheriff. Nobody went in or out since the suspect had gone in. If Ben's bullet had found its mark, the suspect across the street might have lost a lot of blood by now. He might even be unconscious.

It wouldn't hurt to go over and take a look outside the apartment building. I rose from my concealment and walked over in front of the building. There were a few drops of what looked like fresh blood on the concrete by the door. I went into the building and up the stairs. A few more drops of blood led me to one of the apartments.

I put my ear to the door. I couldn't hear any sounds through the door. I put my hand on the doorknob and hesitated. Maybe I should wait for the sheriff to get here. But then I thought there might be another way out of the apartments, like a fire escape. I couldn't watch the front and back.

I slowly turned the knob. I pushed the door open with caution. I didn't see anybody as I stepped into the room. Then for a split second, I felt a hard pain on the back of my head.

The wounded man watched as the intruder to his apartment slowly opened the door. He waited until the intruder had stepped into the apartment before slamming his blackjack down hard on the back of the man's head. As he crumpled to the floor, the wounded man stood over the prone body for several seconds, recognizing him as John Brennon.

If I have the time, I would finish you off to get you out of my hair permanently, he thought, looking down on the body on the floor. *But I don't have the time right now. I need to get out of here.*

The wounded fugitive quickly made his way out of the apartment building and out into the dark night. He needed a place to go for the night—a place where nobody would think to look for him. There was one place he could go for the night. He started walking. He stayed in the shadows as much as he could without being obvious about it. He finally arrived at a two- story house. He knocked on the door. Allen Wing, a man whose friendship Frank had bought in various ways opened the door.

"Frank," he said cordially. "What's up?"

"Can I come in, Allen?"

"Sure. I'm sorry. Can I get you a beer or something to drink?" Allen asked, closing the door behind Frank.

"Yeah. A beer would taste good. Thank you."

Frank sat down on the couch. Even though he had put a pressure bandage on his thigh, blood had still seeped through his pants. It was hard to see because it was just a spot and the pants was a dark brown. Allen returned with two beers and set them down on the coffee table. Then he sat down on the couch himself.

"Have you got a car, Allen?"

"Yeah. Why?"

"I need to borrow it for a little while tomorrow."

"I'll be happy to lend it to you, but I can't until the day after tomorrow. I had to take it into the garage tonight so they could put new brakes on it tomorrow. They said I could pick it up tomorrow at three o'clock. What happened to your car, Frank?"

"It isn't running right now."

"What's wrong with your leg, Frank?"

"What makes you think anything is wrong with my leg?"

"That spot on your pants has gotten a little bigger since you got here. Is it bleeding?"

"Yes. A little bit. Don't ask how I got wounded. I just need a place to stay for tonight. I understand there is a doctor in a small town fifteen or twenty miles from Cedar Falls that will take care of any wound without asking a lot of questions. Do you know the doctor's name and what town he's in?"

"Let me think. I know who you are talking about. I just have to think of his name." Allen was silent for a minute while he tried to remember. "Dr. Bullock is his name. He's over in Ogdon."

That night and the next day, Frank stayed off his leg, allowing it to almost stop bleeding. Around nine o'clock in the morning of the second day, Frank left Allen's house to go to Ogdon. His leg was beginning to throb a little like there might be some infection in it.

Around three thirty, Frank was in front of a large white house that had a sign in front of it that read: Dr. James Bullock, MD. No appointment necessary.

Frank glance around the area as he got out of Allen's car. Everything looked normal, he decided as he walked up to the door. He didn't bother to knock, and just walked right on in.

There was a small reception area that had been furnished with several comfortable- looking chairs. There was an open unmanned counter area. Sitting on the counter was a small bell that someone could ring by hitting the button on top of it. A sign on it said: Ring for Service.

Frank rang the bell. Shortly, a man in his mid-fifties appeared. His thinning gray-brown hair was neatly combed. He wore a white shirt, tie, and white lab coat.

"Yes, sir. What can I do for you?"

"I have a problem in my leg I need you to look at, Doc," Frank said.

"Certainly. Come through that door there, and I'll have a look at it."

Frank went through the door to meet the doctor on the other side. The doctor led Frank to an examination room, where he checked Frank's blood pressure before having Frank lower his pants so he could check his injured leg. He gingerly removed the bandage Frank had wrapped around the wound. The bullet hole was red and inflamed. It had stopped bleeding.

"You have some infection in your wound. Luckily, the bullet went clear through."

"Will you be able to give me something for the infection?"

"Yes. I'm going to give you some antibiotic pills and some antibiotic ointment to put on that. Keep a clean bandage on it, and it should heal fine. If you can come back in a week, I can check it to see how it's coming along. Let me go to my office, and I'll get the pills and ointment for you."

After five minutes went by without the doctor returning, Frank got up and slipped out of the examination room.

He heard the doctor's voice talking in another room. He quickly moved to the door of the room he heard the doctor's voice coming from.

"Hello. Is this the Cedar Falls Police Department? I heard you are offering a reward for information leading to the arrest of your local rapist and killer."

Frank burst into the office, wrapped his arm around the doctor's neck in a chokehold, and took the phone receiver out of the doctor's suddenly nerveless hand and put it back on the phone's base.

"Now, Doc, why did you have to go and do a thing like that? I was told you were very discreet when it came to your patients. How much was the reward for?"

"Five thousand," the doctor choked out.

"Where are my pills and ointment, Doc?"

The doctor picked up a prescription bottle filled with pills off his desk and handed it to Frank. Frank took it and looked at the label.

"How did you know my name? I hadn't told you what it was yet?"

"Several years ago, you were on trial for terrorist activities. I was one of the jury members. I remembered your name and face from the trial.

I made a mistake today. I never should have called about the reward. You have my solemn promise I won't make the same mistake again."

"You're right, Doc. You shouldn't have called the cops. A very bad mistake," Frank said softly.

Denise quickly drove back to the park. Just as she was afraid might happen, the sheriff and other officers had already left. She decided to try the police station next. She got to the station, went in, and asked for the sheriff, knowing he was there because his car was parked outside. She was told he was in conference right now.

"Tell the sheriff John Brennon is very certain he is watching the apartment that has the guy in it that escaped from the park."

"You stay right here. I'll tell the sheriff."

The officer went to a conference room. He was in the conference room for only fifteen or thirty seconds when the sheriff came out and came directly over to Denise.

"What's this about Brennon supposedly knowing where the guy is that escaped from us down at the park?"

"John and I happened to be by the park when the guy escaped. We cruised the area, and we think we were able to follow the guy back to his apartment building. John said he was going to watch the building while I came and got you."

"What makes you think this guy you and Brennon followed home to the apartment is our perpetrator?"

"For one thing, we watched him burst through the bushes at the park. Two, he was dressed from head to toe in black. Three, when Ben shot at the guy, it looked to us like he was hit in the leg. Four, the guy we followed to the apartment building limped just a little when he climbed the stairs to go to an apartment on the second floor. Now, if you don't hustle a little bit, Sheriff, the guy could get away for the second time tonight."

"Okay. I'll follow you over to this apartment, but if this turns out to be nothing, well, I'm not going to be a happy sheriff. Are you sure you still want me to follow you?"

"Yes! We are wasting valuable time."

"Okay. Go on out to your car. I'll get Officer Hollister, and we'll be out in a minute."

Denise went out and waited impatiently for the sheriff and Ben to come out. After what seemed like an eternity, they finally came out of the station. Denise got into her car, and the sheriff and Ben got into the sheriff's car. Denise pulled out with the sheriff right behind her.

She pulled up in front of the apartment building and jumped out of her car. The sheriff parked behind Denise's car. The sheriff and Ben got out of their car and walked up to join Denise.

"Where is Mr. Brennon, Miss Cole?" the sheriff asked.

"He said he was going to stay hidden in this cover here and just watch the apartment unless the guy tried to leave. Then he was going to try to detain him. He would have seen us pull up, and since he hasn't made an appearance, I would say he is over at the apartment building."

"Okay. We'll go have a look."

The sheriff, Ben and Denise walked across the street to the apartment building. When the three of them got to the door, Ben knelt down and examined a couple of spots on the concrete.

"Sheriff," he said, "this looks like it might be blood spots to me. What do you think?"

"Well, it looks like it might be to me too," Sheriff Blocker agreed after examining the spot himself. "We had best be on guard. You said the guy went up to an upstairs apartment, Miss Cole?"

"Yes. We watched him go up the stairs."

Cautiously the sheriff and Ben made their way up the stairs with Denise following. They got to the top of the stairs without incident. They could see the door of one of the apartments was open. They noticed the blood spots on the hall floor leading to the apartment with the open door. The three stopped for a second when they heard a groan come from the apartment. They quickly advanced to the apartment. The sheriff took the top, and Ben took the bottom, covering the apartment's interior with their guns.

When I groaned again and tried to sit up, I found myself looking down the barrels of two pistols. I gingerly touched the back of my head with my hand. I felt a good-sized lump back there. The sheriff and Ben rushed in and started to search the other rooms. Denise appeared at the door.

"John! You're hurt!" she cried. She rushed over and knelt down beside me. She draped an arm over my shoulder to help hold me in a sitting position. "Do you need to go to the hospital?"

The sheriff and Ben finished checking out the apartment and came back into the living room. With Denise's help, I got up from the floor and moved over to the couch. The sheriff sat down in an overstuffed chair. Ben stood at the door to keep any curious onlooker out.

"It looks like Miss Cole and you were correct in your deductions concerning this guy you followed to this apartment. Deputy Hollister and I found a bloody pair of black pants in the bathroom. There is blood in the sink too. But why didn't you wait outside? You realize you're lucky you weren't seriously injured or killed, don't you?"

"Yes, I know. After Denise left to get you, I got to thinking. I could watch the front, but what if there was a back way out of here? I couldn't watch the front, sides, and back all at the same time. And since I was fairly certain Ben's bullet had found its mark, there was a good chance he had lost a lot of blood, maybe enough for him to be lying up here, passed out. So I decided to take a chance and came up. Apparently, he was behind the door when I opened it because I never saw him before it was lights out for me."

Just then, an older man appeared at the open door. He looked around a little then tried to push past Ben.

"You can't come in, sir. This may be a crime scene," Ben said, holding him back.

"Excuse me, Officer, but may I ask what in the hell is going on here? And what do you mean by a crime scene? I don't see any dead bodies lying around."

"And who are you?" the sheriff asked.

"I happen to be the owner of this building."

The sheriff motioned to Ben to let the guy come in. "I live right across the street. I saw you guys come up here, and when you didn't come out after a short period of time, I began to wonder what was wrong."

"Who rents this apartment, Mister…?" the sheriff asked.

"My name is Max Butler. The name of the tenant is David Cumming."

"Does he lease it, or is it a month-to-month rent?"

"Month to month."

"How long has he been renting it for now?"

"I'm not sure without checking my records, but I think four months or so."

"Did he say where he had lived before moving here?"

"No, and I didn't ask either. I didn't see where it was any of my business."

"Was he a good tenant? Did he pay his rent on time every month? Was there ever any complaints of loud music or loud parties from any of his neighbors?"

"He always paid his rent on time in cash. Never had any complaints of any kind about him. Some nights I don't think he was here. For all I know, he might have been out of town on business the nights he was gone."

"Could you describe Mr. Cumming?"

"Not really. Average height, average weight and build. Brown hair. Always clean- shaven."

"Okay, Mr. Butler, I don't think your Mr. Cumming will be coming back. Don't let anybody into the apartment until I notify you. We should be done with it in three or four days. My deputy will be over in a little bit to get the key to this apartment. Thank you for your cooperation. By the way, if Mr. Cumming should happen to get in contact with you, please let me know immediately."

"Whatever you say, Sheriff. Was there anything else, or am I free to go?"

"You're free to go."

The sheriff waited for Butler to leave before turning to Ben. "Hollister, first thing tomorrow morning, get on the phone to Lincoln and request a full forensic team to come and go over this apartment with a fine-toothed comb. Once we get the fingerprints lifted from the apartment, we'll run them through state and federal databases as well as compare them with the other prints we've picked up along the way. We'll leave everything the way it is for the forensic team. Go on over to Mr. Butler's house now and get the apartment key and lock it up.

After the sheriff left, Ben went over to Mr. Butler's house and got the apartment's key. He came back and sat down on the couch beside me.

"Are you sure you don't need to go to the hospital, John?" she asked.

"I'm sure. I'm fine. I have one hell of a headache, but I'll survive. Do you think our man has lost enough blood that he'll need medical attention, Ben?" I asked.

"I think he might have. There was a fair amount of blood on the pants, and God only knows how much he washed down the sink. I'm sure Sheriff Blocker will call the hospital to see if anybody has come in with a gunshot wound, and if nobody has, he will put them on the alert that somebody may come in."

"If he comes up with nothing here in town, do you think he will check Lincoln hospitals?"

"Probably. The sheriff wants this guy in the worst way. He won't leave any stone unturned. We had better go now. I need to get the apartment locked up."

Denise and I walked out to my rental car. We just sat there for a minute, watching Ben get in his patrol car and pull away.

"Are you going to wait and see if anybody shows up at any of the hospitals with a gunshot wound?" Denise asked.

"I don't want to. I think it will be a waste of time. I wish I knew if there was another doctor within a fifteen or twenty- mile radius of Cedar Falls. He would have to be a doctor that wouldn't ask too many questions if someone came in with a bullet or knife wound. I haven't been in town long enough to know the underbelly of the region."

"I don't know any shady characters either, but shortly after I started teaching at the college, there was a freshman who had transferred here from another college. She is in one of my classes. I noticed she appeared to be very sad most of the time. I was able to become friends with her. She confided in me that her boyfriend had gotten her pregnant and then bailed out on her. She wanted to get an abortion, but she couldn't find any doctor here or in Lincoln willing to do it because of the reasons she gave for wanting it done. Then someone told her about a doctor in a small town close to Cedar Falls that would do almost anything for a price without asking a lot of questions."

"Now that sounds like the kind of doctor every lowlife would love to know. Did she have the abortion?"

"Yeah. Afterward, she was sorry she did, but it was too late then. For a while, she was a regular basket case, but I was able to talk to her and help her finally accept that what was done was irreversible. We've remained friends ever since. This is her senior year now."

"Do you think she would remember the name of that doctor and what town he practiced in?"

"Maybe. It's been between three and four years since that happened, but something like that would leave such an impression on you. She might remember his name. I'll get her off to the side and see what I can find out."

"When will you see her again?" I asked.

"I have her in class tomorrow. I'll see if I can't talk to her after class."

"That would be great," I said. "I had better get you home. It's been a long day."

"You're right. It has been a long day, and I am tired."

The next day, Denise kept a close eye on Sue in her classroom. Just as Sue was about to leave the classroom, Denise caught up with her.

"Sue, could I talk to you for a minute?"

"Sure, Denise. It has been a while since we've had a chance to just talk. How did your summer go?"

"Pretty good. I was able to just take it easy and have a three-month vacation. Come on down to my office, where we'll be more comfortable."

Sue followed Denise down to her office. They got seated before Denise took up where she left off.

"I've also been following what has been happening with our latest crime wave." Denise said.

"It scares me to death. I very seldom go anyplace by myself. I won't feel safe until this guy is caught and put behind bars," Sue said with emphasis.

"Well, he was just about caught last night, but he got away. However, he also got shot in the process of escaping. The guy will probably need medical attention, but a friend and I don't think he will risk going to the hospital here in town or even in Lincoln. My friend and I think we know where he will go to get the medical attention he needs. You remember when we first met?"

"Yes. I remember," Sue said softly.

"I don't like to bring up bad memories, Sue, but we think the guy behind the current reign of terror will go to the same doctor that you used then. Is there any possibility that you could remember what that doctor's name is and where his practice is?"

"I know it's only been a couple years ago, but it seems like a lifetime ago. I try not to think about that part of my life."

"And I truly understand what you are saying, Sue. I doubt if I would think about it if the shoe was on my foot. But to make it safe for all women to walk on the streets again, I need that doctor's name. Please."

"Ah. Doctor…Doctor…Bullock was his name. He is, or was, in Ogdon. Please don't mention my name if you do go and see him. I don't want him to have any reason for getting in touch with me."

"Don't worry, Sue. I wouldn't do anything that would hurt you in any way. What happened in the past will stay between you and him. I will be telling the sheriff's office about Dr. Bullock, but I promise your name will never be mentioned. But you can have the satisfaction of knowing that this piece of information may very possible help put a predator behind bars."

"I really hope so. I've got to run now. Take care, and I'll see you in class."

"Okay, Sue. You have a good day now, and thanks."

I was straightening things up in my classroom when Denise walked in. "Hello, Denise. What brings you to my neck of the woods?"

"Hi, John. I talked to that girl I told you about, the one who had the abortion."

"Yeah. How did it go?"

"As you can probably guess, she was reluctant to bring that chapter of her life up, but I managed to impress upon her the importance of her telling me the doctor's name and where he practiced."

"So you're saying you did get the information?"

"Yes. She finally told me after I promised I wouldn't reveal the source of my information to anybody, including the doctor himself."

"Now all I've got to do is figure out an excuse to go see him," I said, thinking out loud. "It would have to be something that a law-abiding, ethical doctor wouldn't want to deal with. I really didn't want to shoot myself to give me a reason to see him."

"You won't have to. You are going to be my brother. I am going to be four months pregnant, and I'm going to be wanting an abortion because I found out my husband is cheating on me. I'm going to be getting a divorce, and I don't want a kid getting in the way while I'm trying to rebuild my life. How does that sound?"

"Pretty good. I think in Nebraska it's against the law for a doctor to do an abortion after the third month unless it's done to save the mother's life. If I were a regular doctor and a woman came in, demanding an abortion with that kind of attitude, I would send her packing so fast she wouldn't know what hit her. But that sounds like something our good doctor would bite on."

"I'll tell him I'm a week into my fourth month."

"What if he doubts that you're pregnant? You certainly don't look pregnant. And it wouldn't do for him to take an x-ray or ultrasound of you."

"First, I'll tell him the women in my family has small babies so we don't show until our sixth month. If that doesn't satisfy him, I'll have to show him an x-ray of a baby in a womb."

"You are just full of surprises. Where in the world are you going to get an x-ray of a baby in a womb?"

"How about my files?" she asked with a smile.

"Why would you have something like that in your files, and how did you get your hands on it in the first place?"

"Relax," she said, laughing. "It's an x-ray of my cousin when she was pregnant a year ago. Her husband's job transferred him out of the blue, and what with getting ready to go, she forgot she had given it to me. I offered to send it back but she said not to. Well, what does your schedule look like?" she asked.

"I can go this afternoon."

"Good. So can I. Why don't I pick you up at the Music Building, let's say high noon? We'll eat lunch at Jim's Cafe and then go out to Ogdon. Do you know where the town is?"

"I've heard of it. I have a state road map at home I can look it up on. I'll know where we're going by the time we leave town this afternoon."

At noon, I picked Denise up, and we had our lunch at Jim's.

"How are we going to get this guy to give us any information?" Denise asked as we left Cedar Falls. "If what we've heard is true, he might not want to reveal anything about his clientele unless the price is right. I don't know about you, but I don't have enough money for a bribe."

"Neither do I. The only thing I know is, maybe I could pump the receptionist while you are back with the doctor. Maybe when he has you in the examination room, you could try to pump him a little."

"That is one advantage a girl has over a guy. She has a variety of charms that most guys are very susceptible to. Which charm do you think I should use, and which ones do you think I should keep in reserve?"

I looked over at her to see if she was serious. She was smiling when I first looked at her, but something in my face told her that she had said the wrong thing. Her smile quickly left her lips.

"I'm sorry, John. I shouldn't make light of things like that, not with what this guy has been doing."

"It's okay, Denise. I know you were just kidding around, and I know you are certainly not the kind of girl who would use her natural charms for any but the most pure reasons. I guess maybe seeing how devastated the one girl was who was almost raped and then seeing the dead girl the other night in the park has really showed me how ugly rape is. Don't get me wrong. I've always thought it was an ugly crime. These two just emphasizes how ugly."

"What do we do if you can't get anything out of the receptionist and I can't get anything out of the doctor?"

"I don't know. As bold as this guy is getting, I would be tempted to break into the doc's office after he's closed, in the hopes of finding something that would help."

"That's how you get in trouble. There has got to be another way. We'll see what happens when we see the doctor."

Shortly we pulled up in front of the house and office of Dr. Bullock. "Well, are you ready to do your thing, Denise?" I asked.

"I think so."

"You have the x-rays from your files?"

"Right here."

We got out of the car, walked up to the office door, and stepped on in. I was surprised when there wasn't a receptionist behind the counter. Denise and I walked over to the counter and rang the bell that sat there. Nobody came to answer the bell—no receptionist, no nurse, no doctor, no nobody. The hair started to stand up on the back of my neck. It wasn't natural for the office to be wide open like this with nobody around.

"Something doesn't feel right here. Keep an eye open out here in the reception area. I'm going to check things out in the back a little."

"Okay. Be careful back there. Things don't feel right to me either."

I stepped through the door between the reception area and the office and examination area. I looked left and right. There was nobody. I went down a short hall, which had four open examination rooms, two on each side of the hall. All were empty. At the end of the hall was a door marked "Private." I assumed it was the doctor's private office. I knocked. There was no answer. I eased the door open while calling the doctor's name as I did.

There were several filing cabinets along one wall. Several of the drawers were open, like somebody had searched at least some of the files in a hurry. A moderate-sized desk with an office chair behind it took up some more of the room. Two comfortable- looking chairs sat in front of the desk.

I went back out into the hall. There was one more door that said "Supplies" on it. I tried the knob. The door was locked.

"Have you found anything?" Denise asked, leaning through the window over the counter.

"No. Not yet," I said, coming up to the counter. "All the examination rooms are empty,and everything appears to be in order. Our good doctor's office files look to me like they had been hastily searched, though. There is a supply room, but it's locked. I would really like to take a peek inside it."

"Check the drawers here at the counter. Maybe there is a spare key for the supply room here," she suggested.

I started looking through the drawers. I found a key that was tagged as being for the supply room. I took the key and went back down to the supply room. It fit, so I unlocked it and opened the door.

Startled at what I found, I jumped back a little. Denise was watching me from the window.

"What is it, John?" she asked quickly when she saw my reaction.

"I think I might have found our good doctor," I said.

Denise's head disappeared from the window. Then she burst through the reception room door and rushed down the hall to where I was.

What appeared to be a lifeless body was laid out on the supply room floor. There was no blood from any wound on or around the body. He was dressed in a white lab coat with a name tag that read "Dr. Bullock," dark pants, and a white shirt with a tie. After a couple of seconds, the shock wore off, and Denise and I quickly moved into the supply room to check for signs of life. I tried to find a pulse in his neck. There was none. Denise tried on his wrist. She came up with the same results.

"What do you think killed him, John? There's no wounds like from a gun or knife."

"It could have been from poison. Remember Gains was killed in the hospital with cyanide. A quick needle to the neck when his back was turned would be all it would take. Or all the killer would have to do would be get his hands on the doc's head and give it a sharp twist. A big guy wouldn't have any trouble breaking the doc's neck. But why kill him? Was he afraid the doctor might turn him in even though Bullock had the reputation of someone a criminal could trust? I had heard around town a couple of days ago that the town was offering a reward for information leading to the capture of the killer. Maybe the doctor here also heard about the reward and decided to cash in on it, only the killer caught him in the act and decided he had to silence him for good."

"That would certainly make sense why he killed him. Maybe Bullock left a note in his office someplace that would tell us who his last patient was."

"Let's take a look. Lock this back up first in case somebody should happen to come while we're in his office. Then we had better get out of here. It really wouldn't be a good idea for someone to find us in here with a dead body."

We locked the supply room back up and went into the office, keeping the office door open. Denise started going through the open file drawers while I concentrated on the desk. The three desk drawers held the usual pens, pencils, stationary, paperclips, etc., that would be found in most desks. The top of the desk held a telephone, a lamp, a small desk calendar, and a large blotter.

"Have you found anything interesting in the files yet?"

"Not yet. So far, all the names are unfamiliar to me. You haven't found anything yet, I assume?"

"I don't know. Maybe."

I had noticed there was an area on the edge of the blotter that was raised just a very little bit. I raised the blotter up. A piece of paper had been pushed under the blotter. I pulled the folded paper out and opened it. The name of the patient and what he was treated for was written on the note. The name didn't surprise me at all.

"What did you find, John?" Denise asked, coming over to stand beside me.

"I found this paper stuck under the blotter. I would take it to be the name of his last patient."

"Why would Bullock stick it under the blotter? He has files on the rest of his patients. Why wouldn't he start a file on Frank?"

"I think he would have later but after Frank had left. He just scribbled this down quickly as a reminder of who Frank was and what he had treated him for. Unfortunately our good doctor never got a chance to put it in his file."

"Doctor Bullock!" a woman's shrill voice called from the reception area.

"Go get rid of her," I quickly said to Denise as I ducked back out of sight. Denise hurried out to the counter.

"Yes, ma'am," Denise said courteously. "May I help you?"

"I need to see Dr. Bullock. I've got a burn on my arm that I need him to look at."

"The doctor is gone on an emergency call right now. I don't know how long it will be before he returns."

"I don't remember seeing you here before. What happened to the nurse that was here the last time I came in?"

"She quit. I'm his new nurse."

"Couldn't you just give me something for this burn? It's hurting some, and I don't feel like driving clear into Cedar Falls. If you can't give me anything to put on it, I'll just wait and hope Dr. Bullock comes back soon."

"Hold on a second. I might be able to give you some ointment for that burn. I'll be right back. Just have a seat."

Denise went back to the supply room. She still had the key to it in her pocket from before. She went in and came back out in about five minutes' time with a tube of something in her hand. She relocked the supply room and returned to the counter.

"This should take care of your burn, ma'am," Denise said, handing it to the woman. "The office will just bill you for the ointment."

"Thank you very much," the woman said and left.

I rushed out of Bullock's office and ran up to the counter as Denise gave a big sigh of relief.

"That was close," I said. "How did you know what to give her?"

"The parents of a friend of mine in New York owned a drugstore. From spending time with them, I learned some basic remedies like for a burn."

"What made you think Bullock would have anything like that on hand?"

"I noticed some medicines on the shelves when we went in to see if he was alive or not. Some of the boxes looked like they might have contained tubes. I gave her an antibiotic ointment that should do the trick. If you don't think there would be anything else to be found in the office, maybe we should get out of here before someone else comes in," she suggested.

"There should be enough evidence with what we've dug up and with what the police has accumulated to bring charges against Frank. He might have already left town after this here, but hopefully, I can catch him before he gets away again. I need you to go to the sheriff, show him this note, tell him what we found here, and try to get him and some deputies to come up to the mansion."

"I'll do my best to get him to see reason. Let's go."

We were quiet all the way back to town. I stopped by her car so she could get the sheriff while I confronted Frank.

Denise quickly drove to the police station and burst into the station. "I have got to see the sheriff right away!"

"What's all the shouting about out here?" Sheriff Blocker demanded, coming out of his office.

"I have to talk to you right now," Denise said again.

"Come on into my office, Miss Cole," Sheriff Blocker invited. Denise followed him in and sat down. "Now what is so important?" he asked, sitting down behind his desk.

"I need you and a deputy or two to come with me to arrest the rapist and killer of the last few months."

"And what makes you think you know who that is?"

"John and I just came from the office of a Dr. Bullock in Ogdon. We found the doctor dead, but before he was killed, he wrote this note," she said, handing the sheriff the note from under the blotter in Bullock's office.

"As you can see, the patient's wound that Dr. Bullock treated coincides with the location of the wound on the killer. I doubt that you have gotten back the DNA report on the blood that was on the pants in the apartment, but when you do get the report, you will find it matches with what they dug out from under the girl's fingernails in the park. John and I also found some cigarette butts in the park that lead right to Frank."

"You do realize I'll have to get a hold of Judge Decker to get an arrest warrant, don't you? And then to get one against a prominent person as Frank Duncan, the judge isn't going to issue a warrant without very positive proof. Most of the proof you have named is just circumstantial evidence with the exception of the DNA, and I can't use that until I get the report back."

"I wasn't aware Frank Duncan was a prominent person in town. I had never heard of him until John found out about him."

"Florence Duncan is a very prominent person, and that carries over to him."

"Look, with all the killing he has had to do lately just to protect his identity, he isn't going to stay in town too much longer. If you wait for the positive proof the DNA test will give you, he is going to be long gone to only God knows where. And John is not going to back down, so Frank will have to kill him to get past him. Are you going to risk another murder when you could pick Frank up on suspicion of murder and then expedite the results of the DNA test? John and I know we aren't wrong. Please, Sheriff, at least go up to the mansion and talk to him if nothing else. I know it's a matter of life or death."

"What makes you think Frank would be at the mansion? That would be the first place we would normally look if we wanted to pick him up or to talk to him."

"I'm sure most of his clothes would be at the mansion. Plus, he can't go back to the apartment he was using. John and I think after killing the doctor, he realized it was going to be too hot for him to stay around here any longer. So the logical thing for him to do would be for him to go back to the mansion, pick up some clothes, maybe switch the vehicle he is driving with another one, get as much money out of the bank as he could, and leave town. And if Frank has a gun, John doesn't stand a chance of stopping Frank."

"Okay. I guess I could go up and at least talk to him. But you aren't going anywhere near there. Go home or go to your office at the college—anyplace but at the Duncan mansion."

"Okay. Whatever you say. Just please get up there."

The sheriff and Denise exited the sheriff's office. He called a deputy and Detective Jerkins over. He explained where they were going but that they would just talk to Frank Duncan. The four of them all left the police station at the same time. Denise hurried to her car, while the police got into two patrol cars. She waited until the patrol cars pulled out before discreetly falling in behind them.

I left Denise by her car and started toward the college. I hoped Denise would be able to convince Sheriff Blocker that Frank Duncan was the rapist and killer. I figured the sheriff would be reluctant to do anything because of who Frank was. I drove up to the back of Florence's Cadillac and stopped. I got out of my car and quietly closed the door. I carefully moved around the side of the mansion to check out the large garage that was located in the back of the mansion.

Frank Duncan was busy loading several suitcases into the trunk of a two-year-old Cadillac that I had never seen him or Florence use before.

"Frank," I said, approaching him. "It looks like you are in the process of leaving to go on a trip."

"Yes, I am. I've been here for several months now. Time for me to move on to greener pastures. I only like to stay in any one place for a short period of time."

"I can understand that. It gets too hot for you in one place after a while, I imagine."

"Too hot?" Frank asked.

"Miss Cole and I just came back from Dr. Bullock's office in Ogdon. We found his dead body in the supply room. We believe you had already been there to see him to have him take care of your leg wound."

"You have no proof that I was anywhere near Ogdon today or any other day. Besides, what leg wound are you talking about?"

"I have proof of sorts. The doc wrote a note that has your name and the nature of your wound on it. You didn't find it when you searched his office because he shoved it under his desk blotter. It was also dated."

"This is all very interesting, but that just proves he knew my name. Now I must really be on my way," Frank said.

"Miss Cole went to the police station with that note while I drove here. I figured you would pick up some clothes before taking off. You don't have your apartment anymore, so this was the logical place for you to come. Do you remember when Doris, that was the girl's name you killed in the park, scratched you?"

When Frank didn't move, I continued, "The police was able to get DNA out from under her fingernails. As soon as they match that DNA with the DNA they got from the blood on the pants that you left at the apartment, they will have all the proof they need to prove you are the killer and rapist that has been running around town."

"I have to go," Frank said, turning to get into the car.

"I can't let you do that, Frank," I said, quickly moving to the car door. "You have managed to escape several times now. This is the end of the road. I'm going to call Sheriff Blocker and tell him you are about to leave town," I said, taking my cell phone out of my pocket.

"You arrogant punk!" he snarled as he suddenly whipped out a revolver from his suit coat pocket. "I've had whole police departments try to catch me. They have all failed. What makes you think one man is going to stop me?"

"One reason is, I know your kind. I know how you think except for a few things. For example, why did you kill the women that you did? You had already had your pleasure with them. Why kill them?"

"The blood, Professor. The blood! I love the smell of fresh blood and the sight of it flowing. But I suppose you can't understand that."

"No, Frank. Thank God that I can't. I wouldn't want to."

"Things was going good until you came to town. That other professor might have eventually figured things out. I had no trouble running circles around the police of this town or any other town. But then you came to town. You had to stick your nose in my business. If

Gains had done his job right, the job that I had paid him to do, you wouldn't be here now, giving me trouble. Now move away from the car. I don't want blood all over it from when I shoot you."

"Have you thought about how you would feel if somebody were to rape Florence?"

"How I would feel if somebody raped Florence?" he asked me back. Then he started to laugh. "It would probably be the best thing that could happen to her. All women are sluts at heart. I just gave them women what they wanted."

"What did I ever do to you, Frank, for you to feel that way about me?" Florence's hurt voice asked from behind Frank.

I had seen her come out of the mansion and walk toward us. It was the sight of Florence that prompted me to ask Frank what I did. His answer completely surprised me, though. Frank moved away from the car so he could look at Florence while still keeping me covered with the gun. It was then that Florence saw the gun in his hand for the first time.

"My dear spinster sister," he said, "you have never had a man—or so you keep telling me. If you had ever had a man, you would know what I'm talking about when I say every woman wants it."

"I may still be a virgin, but I know any woman wants to pick whom she has sex with. What has that got to do with you holding Professor Brennon at gunpoint?"

"Your brother is the person who has been doing the raping and killing in town," I said.

"Shut up!" Frank screamed at me.

"Is that right, Frank? Has it been you?" Florence asked.

"Yes! Yes! It's no big deal. All of them women were sluts. They got what they deserved. I have to finish him off so I have no loose ends, and then I am getting out of town like you've been wanting me to."

"Give me the gun, Frank," she said, taking a step toward him.

"Why would I give you the gun, Florence? I'm going to need it to kill him and then later to protect myself."

"Give me the gun," she said again, wrapping her hand around the barrel of the gun. "I'll get the best lawyer money can buy for you. Just let me take the gun."

"No!" Frank said savagely. "I'm not going to spend the rest of my life in prison just because I got rid of a few sluts. Neither am I going to go to the nuthouse just because some judge or jury says I'm crazy. Now let loose of the gun before you get hurt."

"No, Frank. This has got to stop right here and now."

Frank pulled on the gun, trying to break her grip on the barrel. As he pulled, the barrel swung off me and onto Florence's abdomen. As they struggled for control of the gun, Frank's finger tightened on the trigger. Suddenly, the gun fired.

Florence's body went stiff for a couple of seconds, and a look of shock and surprise was etched on her face. Her body then crumpled to the ground.

Then another shot rang out. Frank's body jerked and was flung back like he had been hit by a truck. His gun flew from his hand and landed on the ground several yards from his still body.

"Are you hurt, Professor?" the voice of the sheriff rang out.

"No. I'm fine," I answered.

The sheriff trotted up from the corner of the mansion to where Frank lay. Keeping him covered, the sheriff felt Frank's neck for a pulse. I figured Frank was dead when the sheriff stood up and holstered his gun.

I went over to Florence. She was conscious, so I gently lifted her head and laid it in my lap.

"The sheriff just called an ambulance for you, Florence. Just relax. You'll be okay," I said softly.

"I'm sorry, Professor. Frank had done things in the past that I never approved of, but I had no idea it was him behind all the trouble we've been having in town. I'm sorry he threatened you, and tell Professor Cole I'm sorry if he had threatened her."

"Don't worry about it. It was Frank that did it all, not you."

"But how am I going to be able to show my face in town after what he has done and everybody finds out?"

"Forget about what everybody else will say. Anybody with any brains will realize you didn't have anything to do with what Frank did. All you have to do is recover from your wound and get back to running the college."

Just then Denise came running over to Florence and me from around the corner of the mansion.

"John! I heard two shots fired. Are you all right?" she asked anxiously.

"Yeah. I'm fine. The first shot Frank fired hit Florence here. The second shot was the sheriff putting Frank down."

"Is Frank dead?" Florence asked.

"Yes. I'm sorry, Florence. I know he was your brother and you loved him, but the sheriff didn't have any choice. I'm sorry."

"So am I. So am I…" she said with resignation.

The ambulance got there then. The crew gently lifted Florence onto the gurney and lifted her into the ambulance. The sheriff came over to Denise and me.

"Well, Professor, I heard enough to know that Frank Duncan was our rapist and killer. I really didn't believe her when Miss Cole came to the station, but I'm real glad she talked me into coming out here this afternoon. You two have a good evening, and I'll see you around town."

"You know, John, there is one loose end we weren't able to tie up," Denise said after the sheriff walked away from us.

"And what is that?"

"We never found any proof of Frank's involvement with the local coven of Satan worshippers."

"No, but I think when Florence goes through Frank's personal effects, she will find his uniform and mask. I think we can safely say the coven will fall apart, and the women of the town can safely walk the streets again."

"Let's go down to Jim's and have a cup of coffee," Denise suggested.

"That sounds real good to me."

The End

ABOUT THE AUTHOR

A man of the heartland who has his fingers on the pulse of what makes people tick from living a middle-income life with a wife and three kids. He would love to have you join him in the complexities of bringing criminals to justice.